PENGUIN ARCHIVE

The Umbi

Tove Ditlevsen

1917–1976

A PENGUIN SINCE 2019

Tove Ditlevsen

The Umbrella

Translated by Michael Favala Goldman

PENGUIN ARCHIVE

PENGUIN BOOKS

UK | USA | Canada | Ireland | Australia
India | New Zealand | South Africa

Penguin Books is part of the Penguin Random House group of companies
whose addresses can be found at global.penguinrandomhouse.com

Penguin Random House UK,
One Embassy Gardens, 8 Viaduct Gardens, London sw11 7bw

penguin.co.uk

Penguin
Random House
UK

First published as *Paraplyen* in Denmark 1952
First published in the United Kingdom as part of
The Trouble with Happiness in Penguin Classics 2022
This selection published in Penguin Classics 2025
001

Set in 12/15pt Dante MT Std
Typeset by Jouve (UK), Milton Keynes
Printed and bound in Great Britain by Clays Ltd, Elcograf S.p.A.

The authorized representative in the EEA is Penguin Random House Ireland, Morrison
Chambers, 32 Nassau Street, Dublin d02 yh68

A CIP catalogue record for this book is available from the British Library

ISBN: 978-0-241-75225-8

Contents

The Umbrella   1

The Cat   20

My Wife Doesn't Dance   28

His Mother   36

Queen of the Night   50

One Morning in a Residential Neighborhood   58

A Nice Boy   67

Life's Persistence   76

Evening   85

Depression   93

The Umbrella

Helga had always – unreasonably – expected more from life than it could deliver. People like her live among us, not differing conspicuously from those who instinctively settle their affairs and figure out precisely how, given their looks, their abilities and their environment, they can do what they need to do in the world. With respect to these three factors, Helga was only averagely equipped. When she was entered in the marriage market, she was a slightly too small and slightly too drab young woman, with narrow lips, a turned-up nose, and – her only promising feature – a pair of large, questioning eyes, which an attentive observer might have called 'dreamy'. But Helga would have been embarrassed if anyone had asked her what she was dreaming about.

She had never demonstrated a special talent of any kind. She had done adequately in public school and had shown good longevity at her domestic jobs. She didn't mind working hard; in her family, that was as natural as breathing. For the most part she was accommodating and quiet, without being withdrawn. In the evenings she went out to dance halls with a couple of girlfriends. They each had a soda and looked for partners. If they sat for a long time without being asked, her girlfriends grew eager to dance with anyone at all, even a man with a hunchback. But Helga just stared absent-mindedly around the venue, and if she saw a man who appealed to her – those who did always had dark hair and brown eyes – she gazed at him so steadily, unguarded and serious, that he could not help but notice her. If someone other than her chosen one approached her (this didn't actually happen very often), she looked down at her lap, blushed slightly and awkwardly excused herself: 'I don't dance.' A few tables away, a pair of brown eyes observed this unusual sight. Here was a girl who wasn't going to fall for the first man who came along.

Over time, many small infatuations rippled the surface of her mind, like the spring breeze that made new leaves tremble without changing their life's course. The man would follow her home and kiss a pair of cold, closed lips, which refused to be opened in any kind of submission. Helga was very conventional. It wasn't that she wouldn't surrender before marriage, but she had it in her head that she would have a ring on and present the chosen man to her parents before it came to that. The ones who were too impatient, or not interested enough to wait for this ceremony, went away more or less disappointed. Sometimes she felt a little pang at those moments, but she soon forgot about it in her life's rhythm of work, sleep, and new evenings with new possibilities.

That was until, at the age of twenty-three, she met Egon. He fell in love with her singularity– that indefinable quality which only a few noticed and even fewer judged an asset.

Egon was a mechanic who was interested in soccer, playing the numbers, pool, and girls. But since every love-struck individual is brushed by wingbeats from a higher level of the atmosphere, it so happened that this commonplace person started reading poetry and expressing himself in ways that would have made his buddies at the shop gape in wonder if they had heard him. Later he looked back on this time as if he had caught a severe illness which left its mark on him for the rest of his life. But as long as it lasted, he was proud and delighted by Helga's carefully preserved chastity, and when they had put on rings and the presentation to her family was over, he took ownership of his property on the prepared divan in his rented room. Everything was how it was supposed to be. She hadn't tricked him. Satisfied, he fell asleep, leaving Helga in a rather confused state. She cried a bit, because here, in particular, she had been expecting something extraordinary. Her tears were pointless, since her path had now been determined. The wedding date was set, supplies were gathered, and she had given notice at her job, because Egon wouldn't have her 'scrubbing other people's floors' after they were married. Her friends were appropriately jealous, and her parents were content. Egon was a skilled laborer, and therefore slightly higher up in the world than her father, who had taught her never to lower herself in this world, but not to 'cook up fantasies', either.

That evening, Helga had no clear premonition that something fateful was happening to her. Even so, she lay awake for a long time, without thinking of anything in particular. When she was half-asleep, a strange desire came drifting into her consciousness: If only I had an umbrella, she thought. It occurred to her suddenly that this item, which for certain people was just a natural necessity, was something she had dreamed of her whole life. As a child she had filled her Christmas wish-lists with sensible, affordable things: a doll, a pair of red mittens, roller skates. And then, when the gifts were lying under the tree on Christmas Eve, she'd been gripped by an ecstasy of expectation. She'd looked at her boxes as if they held the meaning of life itself, and her hands shook as she opened them. Afterward, she'd sat crying over the doll, the mittens, and the roller skates she had asked for. 'You ungrateful child,' hissed her mother. 'You always ruin it for us.' Which was true, because the next Christmas the scene would repeat itself. Helga never knew what she was expecting to find inside those festive-looking packages. Maybe she had once written 'umbrella' on her wish-list and not received one. It would have been ridiculous to give her such a trivial and superfluous thing. Her mother had never owned an umbrella. You took the wind and the weather as it came, without imagining that you could indulgently protect your precious hair and skin from the rain, which spared nothing else.

Helga eventually turned her attention to her role as a fiancée, and, together with her mother, carried out the customary obligations. Yet sometimes she would lie awake next to Egon, or in her bed in the maid's room in the house where she worked, nursing her peculiar dream of owning an umbrella.

A certain image started to form in her mind, which gave her secret desire a forbidden and irresponsible tinge, and cast a delicate, impalpable veil over her expression throughout the day, causing her fiancé to exclaim, with jealousy and irritation, as if he suspected her of some kind of infidelity, 'What are you thinking about?' Once, she answered, 'I'm thinking about an umbrella.' And, with convincing seriousness, he said, 'You're crazy!' By then he had already stopped reading poetry, and he never mentioned her 'dreamy eyes' anymore, which didn't mean that he was disappointed in any way. It was just that now she was a permanent part of his life and routine. She sat through countless soccer matches with him, without ever grasping what it was about this particular form of entertainment that made people shout hurray or fall silent as if possessed.

The image that arose from her memory was this: she was about ten, sitting in the window of the family bedroom, looking down into the courtyard, which was illuminated with a weak glow by the light over the back stairs. She was in her nightgown, and should have been in bed, but she had developed the habit, before going to sleep, of sitting there for a few minutes and staring out into the night without thinking about anything, while a gentle peace erased the events of the day from her mind. Suddenly, she saw the gate open, and across the wet cobblestones of the courtyard, onto which raindrops splashed in an excited rhythm, strolled a pretty, dreamlike creature. Her long yellow dress nearly touched the ground, and high above a profusion of silky blond curls floated an umbrella. It was not like the one Helga's grandmother used – round, black and dome-shaped, with a solid handle – but a flat, bright, translucent thing, which seemed to complement the person who carried it, like a butterfly's radiant wings. It was just a brief glimpse, then the courtyard was deserted as before, but Helga's heart was pounding with strange excitement. She ran into the living room where her mother and father were sitting. 'A lady was walking across the courtyard,' she said softly. Then she added, with awe and admiration, 'She had such a nice umbrella!'

She stood there barefoot, blinking into the light. The familiar room, which lacked anything with a comparable essence, now seemed to her cramped and poor. Her mother looked surprised. 'A lady?' she asked. Then the corners of her mouth turned downward, as they often did when something displeased or bothered her. 'It's that girl next door,' she said sharply. 'It's scandalous.' Then Helga's father turned to her with a flash of anger. 'Why the devil are you sitting staring out the window when you should be in bed?' he yelled. 'Get in there and go to sleep.'

She had seen something that she wasn't allowed to see. Something had been let into her world that wasn't there before. After that, every evening – even though she was an obedient child – she crept over to the window to watch the yellow dress drift across the cobblestones, in all kinds of weather, but always with an inexpressibly sweet and secretive air, and always accompanied by that mysterious umbrella, visible or invisible, depending on if it was raining or not. This vision had nothing to do with the sleepy face that appeared in the neighbor's door frame when Helga knocked to borrow a bit of margarine or flour for her mother, who was always short on the most important ingredients when she was making gravy. And it made no noticeable difference when, one day, this neighbor moved away. For a long time, the child still waited at the window for that long, yellow dress and the buoyant, translucent umbrella. When the nightly passage through the darkening courtyard stopped, she just shut her eyes and listened to the rain splashing against something taut and silky and more distant than all her childhood sounds and smells.

Helga and Egon moved into a two-room apartment that was similar to her parents', and it wasn't far away, either. But it was at street level, and an old wish of Helga's was fulfilled, now that she could sit in her own house and look out at the traffic. She had what she'd never had before – time – and, since idleness is the root of all evil (she was easy prey for sayings like that), this gave her a slightly guilty conscience. Not toward the husband who provided for her but just in general. She allowed herself to become a gentle, self-effacing individual; she exaggerated the few responsibilities she had, and emphasized her frequent visits to her parents and their visits to her. Her in-laws lived in the country, and she wrote to them often, though she only had met them at her wedding.

7

Her letters – which contained detailed accounts of how she spent her day doing domestic duties and got the most out of Egon's salary for everyone's benefit – always ended monotonously with these lines: We are both well and hope the same for you. Your devoted daughter-in-law, Helga.

Every morning she and her mother went shopping, each with a headscarf and a sturdy shopping bag. Her mother shopped for the best cuts of meat at the butcher: men who work hard need a solid meal, she explained. Helga served 'a solid meal' for her husband at precisely six o'clock every evening. But from the moment he left in the morning until that hour, she rarely thought of him. When the shopping and cleaning were done, she sat at the window with some darning that was meant to distract her from the fact that she was sitting there idly, while the people in the street all seemed to have so much to do. From her protected, hidden spot behind the curtain, she observed them with interest and seriousness, the way she had, before Egon, observed all men with brown eyes. She was filled with vague curiosity: Where were they going? Why were they so busy? Although she didn't realize it, she was lonely. She often thought about her mother, because, in Helga's eyes, she was a person, unlike everyone else, who never changed. It was a kind of respite for Helga to be with her mother. Mother and child. Comfort. She loved recalling her childhood. She liked hearing her mother talk about things that had happened. Her mother talked a lot. The sentences streamed from her, forming sturdy frames around distant, blurry landscapes. Often she said, 'You are doing so well. You should appreciate it more, but you always have been ungrateful.' 'Ungrateful how?' Helga asked. Then she always got the story about all the tears she had shed when she received gifts. 'In the end, we were simply afraid to buy you anything,' her mother said. And there in the twilight they sat, shaking their heads at the thought of this unappreciative child who had cried over gifts that would have delighted other children. They talked about this mystery in the same tone one might use to talk about getting over scarlet fever: Good heavens, you were so sick, we thought you might never get over it!

Most of all, Helga loved hearing about everything that was outside the parameters of her own memory: about the first words she'd spoken, when she'd been toilet-trained, and so on – things that did not differentiate her at all from any other child a mother might talk about. Her mother liked to end these stories by getting up and gathering her belongings as she remarked: Well, we won't be seeing those times again, or some similar generalization spoken in a tone devoid of complaint, but that left a small rip in the veil that lay over Helga's innermost being, like the membrane around an unborn child.

When her mother left (always just before Egon was expected home) and Helga waved to her familiar substantial figure for as long as she could see it, then she sat back down at the window without turning on the light. A sadness grew within her and around her. She thought: If only Egon would come home. But when he did come, and filled the small rooms with his noisy company, every enchantment was shattered. Could it be that it wasn't him she was longing for? She walked around quietly, carrying out her housewifely duties, picked at her food like a bird, and said 'yes' and 'no', when her husband's remarks required an answer. Once, he regarded her closely. 'You should have a kid,' he said. 'I damn well don't understand why it's not happening.' Then she blushed, partly at her deficiency in that department, but more because she didn't actually mind not having a child. Her togetherness with her mother allowed the child Helga to live on within her, so it was as if there wasn't room for another one. Sometimes she lied to Egon when he asked if her mother had been over, because for some reason he didn't like her mother to visit so often when he wasn't home.

The days passed without much to distinguish one from the next.

One evening Helga had the food waiting for an hour before Egon came home, and when he did arrive, he was drunk. He threw himself down on the divan, from which he followed her movements through the living room with a watchful, sinister glare. 'What's wrong with you?' he asked suddenly. 'Your face looks all pasty.' She was shocked and quickly put some rouge on her cheeks, but later she got used to his tone. She also got used to making food that was easily reheated, because it became impossible to predict when he would come home. She told her mother about it. 'Egon started drinking.' Her mother seemed to be more uneasy about it than Helga was. 'When a man drinks, it's because he's dissatisfied with his wife,' she declared. And, since she was of the opinion that you could always do something about a problem, she advised her daughter to 'talk it out' with Egon and figure out what was the matter. But Helga had never tried to put herself in another person's shoes; it had never been necessary. Her entire character consisted of a pile of memories without a pattern or a plan. There were a number of pairs of brown eyes, a twilight mood, an immense, undefined expectation, a yellow dress, and an umbrella. There were tears and disappointments, and so many other things, and small joys in between. And there was a man who had opened her pale, narrow lips, and for a few moments made her feel the tug of something unknown and wonderful. There was a voice that had said strange and sweet words to her, and over it all stretched the fine silk umbrella canopy of her childhood and her dreams. This had nothing to do with the man who had started drinking. She thought she had given him as much of herself as he could reasonably expect, and her vague feeling of inadequacy with him was only because she wasn't pregnant, as a newly married wife ought to be. But it seemed to her that, as usual, she expected something more for herself, a kind of surfeit that went only to other, unknown individuals. Not that she blamed anyone for anything – she had never done that, because she knew how unreasonable she was. She had written things on her life's wish-list which were achievable: time to dream, a husband with brown eyes, and a child – the last one for conventional reasons. Her outward behavior had always been dictated by tangible things, so she assumed that it was something concrete that had made Egon start drinking and speaking harshly to her. She nodded thoughtfully to her mother over her tea and promised to 'talk it out' with her husband. But she had already decided it was the lack of a child that was bothering him, and matters no one could do anything about were not proper topics of conversation. Not even with her mother.

That evening Egon came home at midnight. He threw his dirty overalls in the middle of the living room and called for Helga, who was warming up the food.

'I'm fed up to here with it,' he said slowly, swaying on his legs like a sailor. She appeared in the kitchen door, staring at him with her sorrowful, wondering eyes.

'What are you fed up with?' she asked anxiously.

'Everything,' he said, his alcohol breath reeking in her face. 'What do you think I am, an idiot?'

She didn't answer, but pulled back from him a step. Her mind was slow, never fully able to follow a situation, especially a surprising one. Her mind quickened only with memories.

'The food is burning,' she said hesitantly.

He laughed callously.

'I don't want any food,' he drawled. 'I ate already.'

'Where did you eat?' she asked quietly, starting to untie her apron. Her hands trembled slightly. He

The Umbrella

could see that she was hurt or afraid, and he laughed loudly again.

'With a good-looking girl, if you absolutely must know,' he shouted triumphantly. Then he belched in her face, walked into the bedroom and lay down on the bed, fully dressed.

Helga followed him. She looked at him, confused, numb to any clear thought or feeling, as she fumbled for a safe, childlike footing. She whispered, 'I'm going to tell my mother.' But he was already asleep.

Actually, she didn't feel any more hurt by the thought that he had very likely cheated on her than she knew a person *ought* to feel. A husband shouldn't drink, but, if he cheats, that is much worse. Instead of having her usual fantasies, she imagined him with another woman, but it really didn't make much difference. It was only her outer life that he was threatening. It didn't change who she was; her body was the same as before, only with the small difference that it had lessened in value to other men. The words 'other men' hadn't occurred to her since she'd got married. Now, as she slowly undressed, she thought only about that, because she knew that her mother would. Her mother would rationalize that if this husband neglected his obligations to her daughter, then she would have to turn to other men with brown eyes for the pursuit of her daily bread – this idea, that the men absolutely had to have brown eyes, in fact came from her mother. A remark that had stuck: Dark men are goodness itself.

Egon slept heavily beside her, and Helga lay observing

13

him. Despite the late hour, she wasn't sleepy. His chin was relaxed, he had a beard, and he was snoring. This was how one might think about a stranger, not one's husband. Maybe he had been a stranger to her for quite some time – ever since the day she had gone to him with such high expectations, and departed with such deep disappointment, in her own quiet way, without acknowledging it as any great calamity. What does one person mean to another anyway, except when one forces the other to act?

Helga's reaction was strange. The times when she'd stolen a small amount of the household money and concealed it in a little box, originally a jewelry box that she had been given for her confirmation, she hadn't had any particular purpose in mind. Perhaps she had tried to convince herself that it was for Christmas gifts or other things they would struggle to afford. But now she realized why she had saved this money. She smiled suddenly in the dark, and very quietly slipped out of bed and walked to the drawer where she had hidden the box. The moon lit the little room like a false dawn. With the deftness of a thief, she counted the money. There were almost forty kroner. She held them in her hands, smiling gently, redeemed and alone, like a child smiling in her sleep. All she could think of was an open, translucent umbrella with a certain shape and color. She longed for the morning, and her heart pounded fast, the way a woman's heart pounds when she is going to meet her lover. She imagined the street in the rain, and herself wandering beneath this silken canopy. Vague, bright images spread like dandelion tufts across her mind: a house where she had worked, the wife in a dinner dress: Oh, Helga, bring me my umbrella. She had held many umbrellas in her hand without thinking about them. Things outside her world didn't really mean anything to her. Until now. Until she acted.

She slipped back into bed, and her husband reached for her body in his sleep, mumbling something she couldn't make out. Carefully she laid his limp hand back under the comforter, as a hint of a distant tenderness flowed through her. For a second, she felt as much searing emotion as she could ever feel for another person, not including her mother. Recently, Egon had often yelled about getting a divorce, said that he wasn't going to stay married to a broom handle, but words slung at her that way passed right through her as through a sieve. Her parents had always yelled like that when they fought. It didn't mean anything, and she was used to it. All that mattered to her was that the neighbors didn't hear. She was never much for arguing; she just figured that other people were so inclined, and she wasn't. She defended herself in another fashion. There was no way of knowing when it would surface. Maybe Egon had never cheated on her at all, but that didn't matter anymore.

The next morning they both acted as if nothing had happened. That was how their lives were. Helga made her husband's lunch, made him coffee, and kissed him on the cheek as he left. Exactly as usual. Then she went shopping, filled with light, expectant thoughts. And there was no one to tell her that she looked beautiful that morning, in the way that perfectly regular people can, once in a while, when they are feeling happy. She brightened the November day like a pale, delicate morning star, trembling gently and devotedly before it is extinguished. She wasn't the same person that she had been the day before. She was a woman walking into shops looking at umbrellas. It took a long time to find the right one. And she carried it awkwardly on the way home, like a man who isn't used to carrying a bouquet of flowers.

Once she was inside, she opened the umbrella and skipped around the apartment with it. Her joy was pristine. She walked just like the woman in the yellow dress from her childhood. She walked past piles of dirty dishes, through large, bright rooms with palm trees in the corners and paintings on the walls. She entered an illuminated ballroom and remembered her first dance. She lifted the hem of her invisible dress and danced a few steps. The shaft of the umbrella was cool, thin, and strong, something to hold tightly, something to admire, to believe in, to acknowledge. Now she could say to her girlfriends: I bought an umbrella. And it would still be all hers. She shut it, studying the way it functioned: the shiny ribs, the tiny, adorable silk buttons, and the durable yet translucent cloth, against which the rain would someday thrum its melody of forgotten and lost times.

Her ecstasy lasted most of the day. She didn't think

about her mother, she didn't clean, she didn't even dust the furniture. She didn't think about Egon either.

When he returned, unexpectedly, straight from work, she was sitting in the window at her usual spot, with the darning basket, which was empty, in front of her. She smiled at him and stood up.

'I haven't made any dinner,' she said offhandedly, adding as a provocation, which was unlike her, 'I thought maybe you would be eating out.'

He didn't answer, and she ascertained that he was sober, and that he was trying to avoid her eyes. Why? She wanted to tell him about the umbrella and her little swindle. She needed to share her joy with someone. But he looked so terribly ceremonious as he sat himself at the table and cleared his throat. 'I'm sorry about yesterday,' he said awkwardly. 'It wasn't true. I was just drunk.'

'I see,' she said flatly. All day she hadn't given one thought to what had happened the day before. Even now it was strangely difficult for her to think about anything other than the umbrella, but the situation demanded that she say something. She felt embarrassed, as he did, and she stared down at her hands.

'That's all right,' she said truthfully. 'I've forgotten all about it.'

She didn't notice the shadow darkening his face, and she didn't register how despairingly he tensed his whole body toward her. She was a person who didn't come when she was called. She was the one who called when she needed something, in a thin voice, which was easily drowned out by the storm. Besides, it is very rare that two people call at the same time and both get responses. She was content in herself – she even had a bit extra to share – but her husband had pursued her for a long time like a big clumsy animal, while she, agile and light as a scared gazelle, had run from him into a bright, hidden clearing in the woods.

She sat down across from him, small and erect, and again seemed to him both secretive and alluring. As he had a long time ago, he asked jealously and fearfully: 'What are you thinking about?' And, just like back then, her clear, dreamy eyes glided over him as she responded, 'An umbrella.' And then, with sudden animation, 'I bought it, Egon. Do you want to see it?' She was already skipping to the entryway, breathless with excitement.

But he followed behind her and suddenly, angrily, pulled the fine object from her hands and broke it in half over his strong knee.

'There's your umbrella!' he shouted, and she stood for a second in shock, staring at the pieces, at the cleverly formed ribs, and the torn silk.

Then she walked silently past him into the little living room, back to the manageable, the tolerable, the predetermined. She sat by the window as before, finally realizing that this was her place, and that everything was the way it was supposed to be. The colors in her memory mixed together, forming the beginning of a kind of pattern. She realized that she could never be the owner of an umbrella. It was only natural – it made sense that it was ruined. She had set herself up against the secret law steering her inner world. Few people, even once in their lives, dare to make the inexpressible real.

Helga smiled distantly at her husband. It was as if he had suddenly caused some string inside her to vibrate slightly, maybe because he had shown her the limits of her potential before it flowed out into nothingness. She didn't think about it like that. She just thought: This is exactly as if I had cheated on him, and he's forgiven me. And she nodded, seriously and absently, as if to a child who wants to take a star down from the sky and give it away, when he, intensely occupied with screwing a new bulb into the ceiling fixture, said to her over his shoulder:

'You'll get another umbrella.'

The Cat

They sat across from one another on the train, and there was nothing special about either of them. They weren't the kind of people your eyes would land on if you tired of staring at the usual scenery, which appears to rush toward the train from a distance and then stand still for a second, creating a calm picture of soft green curves and little houses and gardens, whose leaves vibrate and turn grayish in the smoke streaming back from the train like a long billowing pennant. You wouldn't guess if they were married or not, whether they had children, how old they were, their occupations, et cetera, just to pass the time. You could see marriage and office work in their expressionless eyes. The man hid his face behind the newspaper, and the woman appeared to have fallen asleep. They sat there every morning and evening, at the times office and factory workers commute. Usually in the same seats in the last train car. Recently there had been a few days when she wasn't there. Maybe she'd been sick. So he had sat alone, and to an observer it didn't make any difference. He had spread his newspaper wide and read it carefully, folded it together neatly, and left it on the seat when he got off. A completely regular office worker in his thirties. It was the cold time of year, so maybe she had had the flu.

He lightly touched her knee. 'We're here,' he said.

It wasn't necessary, because she wasn't sleeping. She got up and took her bag out of the baggage holder, straightened her hat and walked in front of him off the train. He looked at her from the side as they continued down the road toward home. She appeared tired; she always did. She wasn't sick, and she didn't do any more than other women who worked while simultaneously taking care of their houses – less, in fact, since they had no children. But she had taken on the attitude that she carried the burdens of the world. At least that's how it seemed to him, and it bothered him. Recently he had been easily irritated. He tautened his lips to a narrow line and cleared his throat:

'Is the cat still at our house?' he asked.

'I think so,' she said. 'I wasn't going to chase it out into this freezing cold.'

He wrinkled his brow and grew silent. The animal had slowly sneaked into their lives. They had come home one evening to find it meowing outside their door. So she had given it a bit of milk and sent it off. The next morning it was back, and he threw a rock at it when they left. But in the evening she let it inside, because it was below freezing, and it seemed to have no other place to go. In the morning the entire house smelled of cat urine; the creature wasn't even housebroken. It purred apologetically at their legs, and she ran around cleaning up after it, spraying ammonia to get rid of the smell.

Then disagreements started over the cat. He let it out, and she let it back in. When they lay in bed in the evening, they heard the faint meowing outside their front door, and she got up to give it something to eat, while an incomprehensible resentment arose in her husband. 'Don't let it in,' he yelled to her. But in the morning there it was down in the living room, jumping elegantly up onto her lap. She babied it. 'Little pussycat,' she said, 'if only you were housebroken.' The smell made her face go pale as they sat and drank coffee. While she was in the hospital, he was able to get rid of it. Every time he caught sight of the cat near their house, he threw a rock at it, frustrated that he could never hit it. But when she came home, the first thing she asked about was the cat. She stood outside the house calling, 'Here pussycat, come here, baby. Mommy's home again.' And it actually did come when she called, as if it had been nearby the whole time waiting for her. She scraped the snow away from around the front step and brought the creature into their warm living room. As she put her cheek to its fur she had tears in her eyes. 'You sweet little kitty,' she whispered. He hated sentimentality, and he hated dirt and disorder. She could put her energy and care into other things. Inwardly, he was glad she had had a miscarriage. That child would have turned their lives upside down. Things had progressed so steadily in the six years they had been married. They had a house and nice furniture, fine friends, the boss over for dinner once a month. A child would have meant she would have had to stop working, their standard of living would have gone down, their social standing too. He saw it as something to be avoided, and he tried to get her to see the sense in his reasoning. But she harbored a gentle expectation, living in a dream world where dry numbers and computations did not enter. 'A real live little baby of our own,' she said solemnly. 'The house? It's just a dead thing.'

He had thought she was betraying their mutual efforts; she had withdrawn from him and was alone with this strange, foreign body. It was as if she were getting younger and more beautiful because of it, and he felt a kind of jealousy, because he wasn't part of her happiness. In his childhood home there had been six siblings, and he remembered it as one continuous crying fit and quarrel about money, of which there was never enough. Children make people poor.

When did the cat show up? It must have been right after they realized she was pregnant, but apart from that, the two things had nothing to do with one another. One morning she was sick and was driven to the hospital in great haste; the whole thing only took a few days, and then he felt relieved. It wasn't anyone's fault. If they had had the baby, of course they would have figured it out. But it was better this way. He picked her up from the hospital, with flowers, bought out of a vague sense that she needed consoling. But she didn't really register the flowers, holding them awkwardly and tensely in the car on the way home. She let him pat her hand, but it was like a foreign, dead object in his. 'Did you chase away the cat?' she had asked, and he thought it was a strange question, but women didn't really have a sense of proportion.

For a few days he took special care above and beyond the usual. He helped her with the dishes in the evening, and he let the cat come around. Once he even removed its refuse personally. But when she didn't seem to notice his efforts, he stopped and went back to the way he was before. They didn't mention the baby. Just once, while she sat with the cat in her lap, she said, 'So I guess you're happy again?' He defended himself, feeling aggrieved, and over time it seemed to him that in fact he had been the one who wanted to have a baby, and that he was the only one grieving for the loss. Since it didn't work out, he could allow himself to be sad about it. As long as she had her cat, she was happy. But he would put an end to that soon enough. The constant filth.

The smell hit them as soon as they stepped inside. He demonstratively opened all the windows. Now that creature had to go. He kicked it off the chair while she was in the kitchen, and it bolted out to her. He could hear her babbling to it as she poured milk in its saucer. He lay on the divan when she came in with the bucket and ammonia, a scarf around her hair. Cleaning woman, he thought, furious.

But a sudden warmth coursed through him at seeing her bent, flexible back, which surprised him. It had been quite a while. 'Grete?' he said.

'What is it?' She didn't turn around.

'Come over here.'

He got up, standing motionless and abashed before her clear, questioning look. Jesus Christ, he thought, we are married after all. But she walked by him on her

sensible flats and suddenly seemed so unreasonably foreign, as if he had never held her in his arms. But it's not
my fault, he thought, with a smoldering, helpless anger.
Was it my fault it didn't amount to anything?

He stared at the closed door and then noticed the cat
under the desk, following him with its predatory stare. It
was lying there as if hunting for mice, motionless and in
patient suspense. He stood totally still in the middle of
the floor, feeling the same preying watchfulness fill his
own senses. He took a step toward the creature, which
hunched its back and hissed quietly. Then he looked for
something to smack it with, but just as he took his eyes
off it, the cat raced over and jumped out of one of the
open windows. He shut the windows in all three rooms,
one after the other, and then walked out to check if the
front and kitchen doors were locked. Leaning against
the kitchen counter he watched his wife. She was putting meat through the grinder and catching it in her
hands, and leading it into a bowl as it came creeping out
of the little holes like long, bright worms.

Keeping her eyes on her work, she said, 'Where did
the cat go?'

He shrugged: 'How should I know?'

She looked up quickly: 'You let it out,' she said. Her
voice trembled slightly with anger.

'Oh, you have cat on the brain,' he said, attempting
a laugh.

She washed her hands and dried them carefully, finger
by finger, as if she was putting on gloves.

'Go and get it,' she said calmly.

He glanced away. He wanted to say something. There was a lump stuck in his throat, as if he was about to cry. What is the problem? he thought. It's almost like she hates me. With a helpless look he walked past her and out of the kitchen.

'Kitty,' he called. 'Here, kitty.' If the cat comes back, he thought, then everything will be fine. But it didn't come. He searched the yard, and all his anger was chased away by something overwhelming and unknown for which he didn't have the words. He looked between the trees in the snow-covered grass; he was searching for a little cat which brought a load of trouble and no joy; it didn't make any sense. He was a man who always had been led by reason, and who had advanced step by step because of this. He had never had urges to do meaningless things. He had married a pretty girl from a good family; in a few years he would be a manager, and then they might be able to allow themselves to have a child. Grete could stop working – 'Here, Kitty, Kitty' – he pleaded for his life and didn't know why. He was afraid. He was moving in unknown territory; he didn't recognize the woman who was standing in his kitchen anymore, demanding he return with a mangy, untrained cat. He wanted her the way she was before, when he could talk to her about everyday things. He would hold her in his arms and feel the pride of ownership again. Maybe he could buy her with that cat.

It was sitting in a corner of the shed, hissing as he approached. 'Kitty,' he whispered gently. 'Don't be afraid. Come inside to your Mama, come on now.'

It slipped between his legs and jumped in through the open kitchen door all by itself. She had it in her arms when he came in. Tears were falling on its fur. She kissed it on the head, on the paws, and gave it long smacking kisses on its ears. He could see her body trembling. 'Grete,' he said, frightened. Suddenly she let go of the creature, as if she had been awoken from a deep sleep. Then she stared at her hands, which had just been caressing the cat so lovingly. She lifted her head and took a wobbly step toward her husband. Then she stopped and wiped her forehead with the back of her hand.

'Well,' she said, 'I guess I'd better finish making dinner.'

He felt something in his mind soften, and he wanted to go and put his arm around her shoulder, to be close to her in some way. Maybe she expected it; maybe she needed it. But then it occurred to him that the neighbors had probably seen him lying on the ground and crawling around between the bushes, meowing.

He straightened his tie and walked back into the living room. The cat followed, its eyes riveted to him. And though he didn't show it, he was aware of its presence all the time.

My Wife Doesn't Dance

She was on her way toward the door to answer the telephone when she heard her husband's voice – she thought he was napping on the divan, but maybe the telephone had woken him – so she turned around to go back into the kitchen. His words reached her, as if from a distance, through the glass door: *Thank you very much, that's very kind of you, but my wife doesn't dance.*

She stopped and listened, blood rushing to her cheeks, and her heart started hammering as if some danger was approaching. What's wrong? she thought, shaken up. Nothing has happened. Of course he knows I don't dance. Everyone knows I can't. If we're invited out to dance, it's a perfectly natural thing to let them know.

She continued her work in the kitchen, feeling distracted and strangely awkward. She had never tried to hide it from him. It wouldn't have been possible anyway. Ever since he had kissed her for the first time, he must have known, or even before he ever met her. It was something people mentioned whenever her name came up. 'She had childhood paralysis, the poor thing.' But it didn't mean anything to him, apparently – and might that be the real reason she fell in love with him?

28

In his eyes she had never seen any of that horribly considerate sympathy.

She started peeling potatoes with quick, mechanical movements, while at the same time trying to calm herself down: Nothing happened, it was just that I heard it by chance (but would he have said the same thing if I had been in the room?). Who was calling? Maybe an old college buddy who didn't know anything about her. A hollow melancholy enveloped her with an unmerciful darkness she could not escape. Something had changed suddenly, though she couldn't say exactly what it was.

Everyone could see it for themselves, so why should it make any difference that they never talked about it? It followed her everywhere, every day, every minute: on the bus, on the trolley, in the stores, and in the long, long streets, where it was almost impossible to slip unnoticed through an open square or – even worse – past those groups of young people standing on corners after work, whose revealing, watchful eyes tormented her more than anything – but not so much after she had gotten married and therefore was generally recognized as a woman who could be desired and loved, and be someone's partner like anyone else. Did he think about it when they were out together? All the time? Had she lulled herself into a false sense of security here, inside the walls of the home they had created together? Her childhood dream of being like everyone else or just to have any other kind of bodily problem, something that wasn't noticed at first glance – an unhealthy complexion, spindly legs, ugly hands – returned to her. That

kind of thing could be hidden for a time, even from the
husband she loved. Then one day, perhaps during an
argument, she might finally hear that it had been on his
mind the whole time. Then she would feel exposed and
cry, as if her life and happiness were ruined for all time,
even though she could still hide it from those she only
came in contact with by chance or infrequently. But a
woman who limps doesn't get exposed the same way.
She doesn't limp more or less, depending on if anyone
mentions it. It is a fact and visible to everyone, like red
hair or a harelip. Until now she had never tried to hide
it from anyone. And if anyone invited her out to dance,
it was only natural that her husband would point out
that she didn't do that. Perhaps coolly and without emotion, as if, in response to another question, he were just
saying: Our walls are eggshell, the bedroom is blue, and
we've been married for about six months. – It doesn't
change what is already established. Only children yell
'limpy-gimp' and they only yell it at you when you're
a child too.

She had slipped from her childhood torments into the
polite and considerate world of adults. She had succeeded in not thinking about what people said about
her when she wasn't there. Besides, she had been able
to elevate herself in other ways. She could speak on lit-
erature, politics, art, and foreign countries as well as any
man in their circle. She had lived in France for two years,
painting a bit and drawing. She had learned to converse
with all kinds of people and to hold her own in any gathering. But did any of this really interest her, apart from

as a vehicle to draw people's attention away from other women's well-formed legs and normal gait?

She was done with the potatoes, and as she stood with one hand on the faucet and the other swirling around in the pot, it was as if suddenly she didn't have the strength to rinse the potatoes and put them on the stove. She sat down on a kitchen chair and dried her hands on her apron. There she remained completely still, staring straight ahead, as if she were a machine that could continue working for a minute after the power was shut off, but would then stop with a shudder and go dead, indifferent to the shreds of incomplete work wound between its ingenious gears and cylinders.

Right, everyone knows. With her most intimate girlfriends she could talk about it once in a while – and then at home of course, where it gradually became an inevitability similar to her mother's arthritis and her father's perpetual headaches.

But to *him* she had never mentioned it. Sometimes – especially at the outset of their relationship – she felt that he was just about to mention it, maybe to help her, but then she got up and gave him a kiss or asked about something and turned his thoughts in another direction. Perhaps he had gradually begun to understand that he must never bring it up, because it would ruin her illusion that, at least to one person, she was complete, the most beautiful and most loved woman in the world. In this way she had succeeded in separating this curse from their marriage, from her husband's eyes and consciousness, and thereby from her own thoughts – at

31

least in the time she spent here in the kitchen and in the other rooms – a newly married and happy young couple's first home. She had placed her life's great despair outside the door, and only when she left home did the sorrowful black cape wind back around her. Because out in the world nothing had changed – not the impersonal, telling glances from strangers, nor the brazen staring of children.

But now someone had opened the door, and an invisible and icy cold wind blew around her, around her alone, and only she felt it. She didn't know what she should do, or why she had to do something. But she did. The words still echoed in her ears: *My wife doesn't dance*. She felt a powerless bitterness, as if he had lied on her behalf, as if he had been unfaithful. But that kind of thing would have been easier for her to bear, because it was something that could have happened to anyone, something both she and others could grasp, discuss, and relate to. This she couldn't share with anyone, least of all her husband, who was now sitting in the living room waiting for dinner while reading the daily paper.

A cold hate washed over her. He was sitting there completely unaware, waiting for his evening comfort. Blameless. But if you feel betrayed, you *are* betrayed.

She got up and went back to preparing the meal. She sliced up the meat, made gravy. Hate penetrated her mind like a bright, sharp flame, forcing her thoughts so far from their usual channels that it was as if a completely different woman were standing there from the one who, just half an hour or less before, had gone into the living room to answer the phone. In this cutting, cool light she saw the form of a strange, inconsequential person, who admired her intelligence, enjoyed her food, and venerated her social class, which was above his. How courteously he had approached her parents' large, solid rooms as a working student, striving for entrance into the culture in which she had been born and raised. Had she ever been anything for him other than a means to achieve a lasting separation from the social class to which he belonged? So he accepted the leg in the bargain! Apparently he wasn't able to conquer a girl who was both cultivated *and* graceful.

But hate is just as void of sense as love. Its fire is cold, burning with evil. There was another man, a shadow of him, and she had to try to make him appear in her mind now, the one who had elevated her to the light with his gentle voice and his good, warm hands, protected her, made her forget. He mustn't notice anything. Maybe (with a tiny, futile wisp of hope) in a little while everything could go back to how it was. She would carry out the food and ask, in a perfectly normal voice, who was on the phone. It would be strange if she didn't ask; it would arouse his suspicions. Suspicions of what? She could say with a little smile: I heard what you said, that I don't dance. But I *can* dance actually, even with the bad leg. Maybe, maybe then everything would be even better than before, when there would no longer be anything between them that they couldn't mention.

And she told herself that he wouldn't love her any more or less than before, since he did marry her, after all – and everyone knows he did it *despite that*. The hate, and its painful and false vision, slowly disappeared. Maybe he had said it that loudly to actually help her? But the thought that he might have known her anxiety about the subject all along filled her with incomprehensible shame, which was more unbearable than everything else.

She drew out her tasks, feeling almost like a dominant enemy was awaiting her, out in the cozy living room. She had to go in and set the table, but how could she look him in the eye and act naturally?

In a panic, she put the meat on the dish, set the plates on the tray, forgot the salt and pepper, and walked down the long hallway, listening for her own footsteps, her limping footsteps, which he now heard approaching, just like every other evening, and yet not like any other.

He put down the newspaper and smiled at her. 'That smells good,' he said. She started setting the table without looking at him. She formed the sentence privately, the difficult, meaningful sentence: I heard the phone; who was it?

She tried to buy herself some time. While we're eating, she thought, while he's occupied with the food – then he won't look at me.

She went out to get the glasses and felt his gaze glide mercilessly over her body, making her movements stiff and awkward, so the shorter, skinny leg hobbled more obviously than usual down the hall. Tears burned her eyes, tears of hate and shame, which could never be alleviated by crying.

When they were sitting across from one another, he cleared his throat as if he were going to say something, and he looked at her, surprised and questioning. Without thinking, in fearful panic, she pushed the water pitcher and it toppled, spilling water all over the tablecloth.

'What are you doing? Wait a second, let me help you.' His voice was friendly, a bit curious, and she let him fetch a rag as she sat motionless, watching him dry the spill carefully, while her heart shrank to a little hard lump. He has no idea, she told herself. He doesn't have any idea what I'm going through. And suddenly she perceived him as a complete stranger, a person she just happened coincidentally to be in the room with, and she was able to feel disconnected from him, from her love for him, her solidarity with him, and she decided again from her profound loneliness to ask who had called – she had already opened her mouth when her eyes met his. His eyes were good-natured, sad, and wise. They were searching penetratingly for something, maybe just a confirmation. Of what? The words stopped at her lips. They would never be spoken.

She smiled sadly and distantly. It's over, she thought. Not yet, not tomorrow. Maybe he'll never know it's over.

'I'm a little tired today,' she said apologetically, and they both started eating, while carefully avoiding looking one another in the eye.

His Mother

The old lady was awaiting a visit. But it's not really accur-
ate to call her a 'lady', although she would certainly find
the title appropriate. Because the term 'old lady' auto-
matically brings to mind a lovable, mild-mannered,
white-haired woman, or at least a dignified one. But lovable is not the right description; mild-mannered doesn't
fit either. And she really is too short, bent, and slovenly to
be called dignified. If you happened to see her apart from
her dreary, stately furniture in these carpeted rooms with
which she has merged, and which soon will be located in
her son's bright, new home, looking awkward and being
about the only things that miss her, you would simply
think: There goes an old woman; or maybe even: There
goes a *poor* old woman, because for years she has never
spent money on herself, except for that pot of a hat she
bought for three kroner last year at a second-hand shop,
and the strange dress she got an elderly seamstress to
make out of her husband's twenty-year-old overcoat
for five kroner (she has a knack for finding cheap labor);
and in addition to that, a kind of smock that was made
from the lining, with sleeves from an old, moth-eaten
curtain. – And she hopes she doesn't have to buy any
more clothes in her lifetime; you get nothing for your

money these days, and who does she have to dress up for anyway–

It was Sunday, and she was expecting her youngest son, who was a student and actually lived at home, but most nights slept at his friends' houses. He was twenty-seven, and his studies were being drawn out, since his father had died completely unexpectedly and left only the bare minimum to support his widow and nothing at all to his son. So he had to work during the day and study at night. An advance on his inheritance was out of the question. Despite her piousness, his mother hated anything that reminded her that she was going to die one day, and the word 'inheritance' filled her with images of ungrateful children, indecent funeral banquets, powerlessness, and darkness. It was good for him to support himself, she thought. Young people shouldn't have inordinate amounts of free time–

But he still had time for girls, however he managed it.

She carefully whisked a feather duster over her husband's portrait, around which hung a dried wreath of small blue and yellow flowers with shiny beech leaves jutting out. She paused in front of the picture, and for a moment merged so silently and naturally with her surroundings that she seemed closer to death than when she was asleep. Then reality again took hold of her sinewy, though fragile body; she shivered, seeking respite from the relaxed, almost jolly eyes above the pastor's ruff collar. 'Young people don't grasp the seriousness –' she said heavily. 'No humility toward life, no sense of responsibility.'

She was really hoping they could keep their hands off one another until they were married. She would never forget that terrible day when she had found something in the inner reaches of the boy's wallet, something about the use of which there could not be the least doubt, even if one had been married to a pastor and quietly received the children it was God's will they should have. She had waited for him tearfully that evening, with the small, sterile, crinkling package between two fingers. 'Now, Asger, have you sunk so low that you don't trust your mother anymore?'

Her eyes grew dark with anger at the memory, while the porcelain trinket on the desk got a once-over with the duster. Then she lugged a chair beneath the crystal chandelier, and, panting heavily, lifted her dress to reveal a pair of short, thick, bowed legs in black socks. She stepped up onto the chair from which, with the help of a surprising ability to stretch, she sent a rag twisted around the end of a broomstick in the direction of the faintly chiming pendants, allowing her to shake down a bit of dust onto the crocheted table cover that had been placed over the large, round mahogany table for the occasion.

He was supposed to come at three o'clock with his girlfriend. Now it was almost four.

She stepped down gingerly and stood there leaning on the broom handle, looking around the living room to see if there were any more specks of dust visible to her weak eyes. She caught sight of her sister's stern, stiff expression, which from several ages and different photographic projections observed the room from all angles. And she sighed long and deep at the thought of the treatment the poor woman had likely been exposed to at the mental hospital, without anyone ever knowing, because she was no longer able to liberate a single thought from her depression's impenetrable morass. 'Poor little Agnes!' But then her thoughts shifted to this sister's numerous offspring, of which the eldest, whom she hadn't actually seen since he was tiny, was at that moment suffering from a terrible pneumonia; and even though nowadays there were treatments for it, you could never know for sure. God's ways are beyond our comprehension.

The old woman's life was replete with misfortunes, the most recent one always seeming to her the heaviest to bear. She sniffed them out and took them in with real talent. Her family was large, taking into account her siblings' children and the families by marriage. And somewhere along the line there was always a still-born baby, a grown son who went off the rails, or a daughter who had a child outside of wedlock. And in some magical way she always knew instantly, and every time it pained her deeply and was just as difficult and burdensome. Alas, what we have to go through – it's a good thing Daddy's not alive anymore! It was really remarkable what she could endure. Even the neighbor's sorrows and the other miseries on her periphery, which she uncovered through conversations with salesmen and residents in her building, hit her hard and painfully. But in the end it all merged together, and at heart she didn't feel noticeably worse when her sister, in her breakdown, completely lost the ability to communicate with other people, than when she heard that the child of a female family member (whom she had never seen) had crashed his bicycle and broken a leg.

When the key was in the lock, she put her hands to her heart, as if she were awaiting some message about the death of a close relative. Oh, dear God, she mumbled, skipping out with quick, tiny steps, tilting from side to side on her short legs, to the kitchen to turn off the tea kettle, which had been put on the gas an hour before and was almost boiled dry. The kitchen was full of steam. Moaning quietly to herself as if there were a fire, she hitched up her dress and crawled up onto a kitchen chair, then stretched the broom handle over the counter to push open the window, even though she knew she couldn't reach to hook the window latch, and she had already broken several panes this way–

He followed her into the dim room awaiting them, and her clear, cool eyes whisked away any creepiness or melancholy. Old junk, they noted, apart from a pretty olive-green corner sofa and a finely carved sewing table. God knows if she would part with any of it if we get married, she thought. What does an old woman like her need all this furniture for?

Suddenly his mother was on her like a cold draft. With embarrassing cordiality she pulled her down and gave her a damp kiss on both cheeks. 'Hello and welcome. I hope you will make yourself at home.' But her voice was plaintive and sad, as if she already foresaw that this person would not only be miserable in the subsequent hours, but that her visit could even cause new problems of unpredictable consequence.

The young woman, who otherwise was rarely embarrassed, felt immediately awkward as she stood there towering over the little old woman, whose brown gaze crept slowly up her youthful form from below, like a wingless insect, slightly diminishing her youthfulness as it made its way up, until the two pairs of eyes met, giving the young woman a vague, overwhelming feeling of anxiety, while a strange attempt at a smile dissolved the mother's heavy, changeable expression. 'Yes, yes,' she sighed. 'It's probably best we use the familiar form of address. Sit right down and I'll make us a cup of tea' (even though we doubtless will die first, before we get that far).

Asger nodded encouragingly to her as she sat down on the piano bench with her back to the piano. He sat in the rocking chair by the window. That old woman was his mother; she had nursed him once. She had actually been young, though this was impossible to imagine. He had blue eyes, there was always a smile quivering around the corners of his mouth, and she loved him. He wasn't at all like that sad, old woman, not at all. He had crawled on this furniture when he was a child. He saw the things here in a totally different way than she did. Naturally. On the wall between the windows hung a painting of him as a child. She pointed at it.

'You were such a cute boy.'

'I look like my father,' he said, glancing at the

flower-encircled portrait over the desk. 'Don't you think?'

She got up and went to examine the man's bright, friendly eyes, which put her in a good mood again, because it was quite true that he resembled his father. She walked over to Asger and ran her fingers through his thick brown hair. It was hard for her to keep away from him for very long.

'Is your mother always so – so sad?' she asked carefully.

He thought about it. Then he said, by way of explanation:

'She's from another era. You have to realize she could almost be my grandmother. My oldest brother is nearly fifty.'

He laughed and nodded toward his father's portrait:

'There was life in the old man,' he said.

She laughed too, and looked at her watch. The sun was out. Right outside. It seemed as if its rays reached the windows with the best of intentions, but then had to give up, slide down the wall in vain, and return to space. But maybe the sun came through in the mornings.

The child of an old man, it occurred to her, as she remembered a phrase from some poem: *born of tired loins*. Her own thought shocked her so much she was compelled to go and kneel in front of him, put his head in her hands, and observe his beautiful mouth and his tired eyes with the distant look in them, and his slim hands which could never be still, so were constantly fumbling with a pipe or cigarettes or searching for tobacco or change in all his pockets. He was so forgetful, a bit hesitant in his manner, like a person who never has all his senses in the same place where he actually is.

He didn't kiss her. He glanced nervously at the door.

'Watch out,' he said quickly. 'Here she comes.'

He jumped up and took the tray from his mother. It was so big and heavy, it was a wonder she had gotten that far with it.

The young woman got up too, blushing slightly, and started setting out the cups, while his mother sat down, recovering from the exertion.

'Asger,' she whined, 'would you mind attaching the hook in the kitchen window for me?'

As he left the room, it was evident from his back that he felt he was being watched, and she felt a sudden tenderness arise within her over his charming awkwardness, his dreamy, idealistic view of life, and his amazing ability to feel joy over the most insignificant things; also the wrinkles around his eyes when he smiled, which he evidently got from his father, since his mother didn't seem able to smile – I mean, had she ever laughed in her whole life?

She smiled uncomfortably at the old woman, who nodded slowly and sadly back at her: 'Well, we have to hope it will lead to a blessing this time,' she intoned.

'Yes,' said the young woman quietly, and a shadow passed through her impressionable mind. A reflection from the eyes across from her, so filled with misery, reached her own open and questioning gaze, and a speck of invisible dust settled on her features, as if for a moment she had merged with the silent horde of photographs which spent their shadowy lives here on the furniture and the windowsills, where no flowers seemed to thrive.

His mother poured the tea when Asger returned. She had dirty fingernails, just like him. But with him it was from all that fidgeting with his pipe, or maybe forgetfulness – at any rate, it didn't matter. But an old woman, she thought, should at least keep herself clean.

The three of them sat around the large round table, so far from one another they had to rise in order to reach the plate of cookies or the fine blue sugar bowl. The young woman's bare summer legs were cold, and appeared pale next to the old woman's dark gypsy-brown skin. Asger took two sugars, and kept stirring his cup long after they had dissolved. It was necessary to say something to him several times before he turned his gaze from the distant point it dwelled on, and looked straight at the person who spoke to him. 'Sorry, what did you ask?' She tended to find this endearing, and she jokingly waved her hand back and forth in front of him, like a person does to see if the other is conscious or not; but even that wasn't always enough to bring him back. Back from what?

He was bored visiting his mother. Naturally. It was morose. She reported on her recent calamities with a dark, droning voice: the little girl who had fallen down the kitchen stairs the other day, and her sister, who was no longer able to communicate. 'But she's not insane, because it's obvious she recognizes me; still, being in such a horrible place must make her feel even more miserable!'

Asger smiled gently.

'Aunt Agnes has always been a bit strange,' he said.

He showed a good appetite, while the young woman sat agonizing over her tea. She felt nauseous. This happened to her sometimes, from hospital smells, for example. She asked Asger for a cigarette and sucked the smoke eagerly into her lungs as if it were fresh air.

'Oh, you smoke too,' said his mother, horrified, and suddenly the young woman looked at her with hardened eyes and thought: You are not going to take him away from me – feeling surprised at herself, because of course there was nothing in the world that could prevent her from loving Asger or that would turn his heart away from her.

The photographs stared into the room. Yellowed, half-faded men with high collars and full beards, and modern, artistic child portraits with embellished chiaroscuro effects. Dark and light eyes, serious and smiling faces, some with the same brooding, heavy expression as Asger's mother, others with hollow, expressionless eyes, as if they were observing the furniture they had once touched and sat on, from somewhere on the other side of the grave. Soon she would be among them, know them, and consort with them. And her children would belong to this heritage for all time and resemble them in some way.

His mother rose and started introducing the family, the dead as well as the living. On the beautiful sewing table were her three daughters-in-law, smiling, slightly apart from the others, as if they were shying away from the rest of the dusty crowd. One had a good-natured, round face with glasses. They probably came to visit often on Sunday with the sons and their children. They knew the round table and the old woman's kisses and moans; maybe they even laughed at her, remembering the first time they were here, when she had terrified them, young and in love as they were. Space could probably be made on the sewing table for another photograph, and on the piano for a couple of grandchildren.

Asger sat in the rocking chair filling his pipe, while his mother bustled about, presenting the pictures. He was probably impatiently waiting to leave, but controlling himself, as one does with parents. 'I'm her last one, you know,' he had said, 'so she still thinks of me as a child.'

'And then here is Aunt Agnete, who died last year. She suffered so much at the end – and here is my eldest son; he's a doctor in Holstebro.' The doctor had an ill-defined, limp mouth, and eyes so pale that in the picture they seemed to have no expression. Did he look like his mother or his father? The next one, a teacher in a community college, definitely resembled the mother, but in a refined, melancholy, weary way. The brown eyes stared out questioningly at the young woman.

'He doesn't look like Asger,' she said, unbelievably happy that he didn't; she wasn't sure why.

She peered over at the man she loved. He was sitting with his ankles crossed on top of the table with the photos of his three sisters-in-law, and he was reading the newspaper, from behind which blue pipe smoke rose.

His chin came to a sharp point before merging into his neck – a sign of character and steadfastness. Yes, his chin did do that–

The gallery was endless. Outside the sun was shining. She was going to suggest to Asger that they go for a walk in the woods afterward, then they could lie on his jacket and look up into the fine, bright greenery until the late twilight coolness forced them closer, and he would warm her with his healthy young body and rid her of her strange anxiousness, and promise he would never take her to visit his mother again, or, at any rate, only on birthdays and similar occasions, when other people were there too. Actually, he could come over and help her out a little, instead of just retreating and sitting there. Suddenly she felt irritated at how he always made himself comfortable wherever he went, not because he enjoyed being there, but because of something else in his personality, something no one could penetrate, and which was always with him. At first she had thought it was only when he was with her that he had trouble pulling himself away, but even when they went to the movies it was a struggle for him to get up and leave when the film ended. He was aware of it. He said it was a kind of inertia.

'And here is Aunt Agnes, whom I mentioned before. This was taken just before she was admitted for the first time.'

The young woman glanced from the mother to the picture and quickly back again. She didn't see any difference.

'She looks so much like you,' she exclaimed.

The old woman nodded solemnly.

'We do resemble one another quite a bit now, both in mind and body, but that hasn't always been the case.'

She tottered over to the desk and fished out of a drawer an old faded photograph of a young girl, a very pretty young girl with a blond top knot and a narrow velvet band around her bare neck. Her forehead was high and broad, her eyes brown and slightly slanted, her mouth on the verge of a secretive smile.

'This is Agnes at twenty-two.'

The young woman hesitantly took the picture in her hand and stared at it. Then she said into the air:

'Incredible how she looks like – I mean, there is such a resemblance to –'

Then a sudden chill crept up from her legs, and both women glanced over at Asger, who was cleaning his pipe, oblivious to their attention and conversation. The old woman nodded. 'I know, there's something around the mouth,' she said, vaguely triumphant, or maybe just with the kind of satisfaction all parents feel upon seeing their own features replicated in their children. She looked intently at the young woman and repeated, slightly louder: 'There really is a striking resemblance around the mouth.'

And his beloved couldn't understand it, and didn't know why it was so unsettling. She didn't even know if that was the cause, or if it would still affect her when she had left the room and its atmosphere, but an anxiety she had never before experienced in her life wrapped unmercifully around her like a cloak, when she admitted that the young woman in the picture – the one who later went crazy – had a small, weak mouth with tiny smile wrinkles continuing out to her cheeks, just like Asger.

He took a deep breath when they were out on the street.

'So, was it bad?' he asked, tenderly teasing, and adding, when she didn't respond, 'We had to get it over with – so what do you want to do now? Is it too late to go to the woods?'

He was in a great mood. He had gotten through something unpleasant. But the young woman looked askance at him with tears in her eyes for that mouth she had loved, which was now ruined for her. So far, just that.

Then she said, 'You know what, I'm kind of tired. I think I would rather go home.' And she had to hurry home to be alone, before the tears really started flowing – tears over something that maybe wasn't completely broken, but would still never be the same.

Up above, from behind the curtains, his mother stood watching them, motionless and unseen, her eyes dark and imbued with emotion. In her hand she was still holding the picture of her sick sister.

Queen of the Night

While her mother powdered her face and pulled the white angel-hair wig down over her forehead, Grete held up the mirror for her.

Grete was kneeling on a chair, leaning in over the table from the other side, staring from behind the mirror with open mouth and wide eyes, round and shiny with excitement.

'That looks so great,' she said.

Her mother whispered nervously, 'Ssh, you'll wake Daddy.' She wrinkled her forehead while applying a thick, greasy pencil to her eyebrows. Then she turned her head and peeked in the mirror to see how far into her temples the line should go. Her skin looked brown as coffee against the white wig. Grete put out her hand.

'Can I touch it?' she whispered.

'Hold the mirror up for me.'

Grete pulled back her hand.

'Oww,' she said, surprised.

The white artificial hair hurt her fingertips.

Her father stirred on the sofa behind her, and both of them went stiff until he settled down again.

Grete sat up on the table, because it made her belly hurt to hang over the edge. Next to her lay an orange lipstick, to go with the white hair, and a little case with black eyeshadow, which was wet in the middle from spit. Black and red and white and silver. Her mother's costume made a nice crinkling sound when she moved, and she smelled nice too. Her father lay there sleeping behind her. He had to work a night shift, and her mother had to make sure to be home early in the morning before he got off work. Karneval festivities might last all night, but a man could never understand that. Men didn't go to Karneval. There were some pictures of men in the magazine where her mother had found the pattern for her costume, but they just looked foolish. Men went to work, and when they were home they slept. Karneval was for ladies.

Grete was glad she wasn't a boy.

Finally she was able to put down the heavy mirror and admire her mother, who was standing in front of the sideboard, holding up the black tarlatan gown with both hands to see if the skirt could be taken off over her head. Grete blushed at how pretty her mother looked. Nothing on her neck or shoulders, and the rest a profusion of eleven yards of billowing tarlatan at one krone per yard (but to her father they said it cost half) with glimmering silver sequins strewn all over. Every single one was sewn on by hand, and they glistened in the light from the bare bulb in the ceiling when she turned – slow and rustling, fragrant and unreal in the modest living room.

She smiled at her daughter, careful not to wrinkle her makeup.

'Do I look fine?' she asked.

Grete nodded eagerly.

The costume was called 'Queen of the Night'. It was the nicest one in the whole magazine. Last year her mother was 'Coachman from the 1800s' in blue and gold satin with a high, black, cardboard hat and boy's knee pants. The cloth for that one had only cost two kroner, but her father, as usual, still had to calculate how many bags of oatmeal or pounds of carrots could have been bought with the money. What nonsense. They had oatmeal and carrots to eat anyway, and her mother didn't get many chances to enjoy herself, and it wasn't her fault he was unemployed half the year, so she had to go out and clean for other people.

Grete was completely convinced they would be better off if her father wasn't around, because he was the only one who put her mother in a bad mood – apart from when the other wives in the building gossiped about her. They were quick to judge. Her mother said they were jealous because she was still youthful and wasn't going to give up every pleasure just because she had a husband who didn't like to dance. When Grete turned fourteen, her mother would take her to Karneval. That was in four more years. Then she would be 'Queen of the Night', with a beauty mark on her cheek and white silken hair. And maybe a black fan. Grete had been up and down the whole street to find one, but the Karneval stores only had colored fans left. In the magazine it said the fan was meant for 'Carmen', but her mother liked it when there were accessories to her costume. Tonight she would have to be satisfied with a little black silken bag she had gotten from a place she had worked, and then of course the half-mask with the fringes over the mouth.

Her father opened his eyes. He hadn't actually been sleeping at all, because he usually awoke very noisily. They noticed him lying there watching them, and her mother's smile disappeared while Grete sat down and started rotating a toy ring around her finger. Her heart was hammering in her chest.

'Look at you,' he said with a gravelly voice. 'You look like a Christmas decoration. People are going to make fun of you, you old scarecrow.'

Grete's back hurt, as if someone had hit her. Her vision went blurry with hate for her father. She pressed the ring's metal setting into her index finger, which made a white mark that slowly turned red. She didn't dare move, afraid that her mother wouldn't make it out the door in one piece. She heard her mother's breathing behind her.

Her father sat down on the edge of the sofa and felt for his slippers underneath it with his feet. There was crud on his face in the two wrinkles that went from his nose to his mouth. He didn't take his eyes off her mother.

'You should go to work like that tomorrow,' he said mockingly. 'You might be able to take a taxi there, if you can find someone crazy enough to pay for it.'

Her mother didn't answer. Grete heard her go out to the entry and put on her jacket. The mask was still lying on the table, but Grete didn't dare bring it to her, for fear of drawing her father's attention. If only he could fall down from some scaffolding and die – or drown – in a marl pit – then everything would be fine.

Tears dripped down on the bare, stained tabletop. Grete bit her knuckles and tried to think about Karneval. About the 'Queen of the Night' in a flood of lights and with all the other cupids and dancers and Carmens like graceful shadows around her. A shiny parquet floor and the melancholy quivering of violins. The 'Queen of the Night' glides dreamily across the floor with a soft, far-away look in her eyes. Sequins like moonlight sprinkle in her wake. She takes Grete by the hand and leads her into the light–

The front door slammed shut, and quick steps retreated down the stairs.

Grete cautiously turned her head to see her father sitting on the sofa staring vacantly into the room. She stood up and started to clean up after her mother. There wasn't anything to be afraid of anymore. There never was when she was alone with her father. Sometimes he tried to entertain her a little, but of course he knew nothing about dresses, lipstick, or dancing. He wanted her to read Grimm's *Fairy Tales*, but they were too boring and only for little kids. She liked the novel series in *Family Journal* a lot better. It was about a young girl who didn't know if the young men were attracted to her for her money. And then one of them apparently put poison in her food, but that would be explained in the next issue. Her mother read it too. It was completely different from reading about fairies and trolls, which didn't even exist!

In the shelter of the mirror, Grete let the

orange-colored lipstick glide over her lips, and she lifted her eyebrows and smiled coyly at her reflection, with her head at a slight angle. She teased out her hair, wondering how it would look if she got a perm. Her mother had promised her one the next first of the month, when she would get a pay rise, but her father mustn't know about it. She put her hand over her mouth and giggled at the thought. Then she cast a sidelong glance at her father. He was still sitting in the same position, bent forward with his big hands clasped together as if he were greeting himself.

Grete got up from the chair and walked over to him.

'Daddy,' she said hesitantly.

He looked at her. Strangely. Almost as if he couldn't remember who she was. His eyes were kind of sad. But he could just stop being so mean to her mother. And not say that she was an old scarecrow!

Her heart felt tight because of his eyes. She turned away and started collecting pieces of cloth and sequins from the floor. She picked up one of them. It was just a piece of bent metal.

Her father stood up and looked at the clock. He cleared his throat.

'Well, I guess I've got to get going,' he said in a completely normal voice, and Grete breathed a bit easier, regretting the marl pit. But why did he always scare them so much? You couldn't ask him about anything or talk with him the same way as her mother, who told Grete everything.

He started putting on his boots.

'Aren't you afraid to sleep alone?' he asked, with the strange, shy voice he used when he was trying to be nice to her, even though he was mad at her mother.

Grete pushed her hair back and smiled bravely at him. She was still a *little* scared, even though it was silly to feel that way.

'No,' she said intrepidly. 'When you're asleep, you can't be afraid.'

Her father laughed hoarsely, and something bright arose inside Grete: Just imagine if he could always be nice and in a good mood.

Then he put his packed sandwich in his pocket and awkwardly stroked the girl's hair.

'What do you want to be when you grow up?' he asked.

'Queen of the Night,' she shouted with excitement, but bowed her head as if from a blow when she saw her father's expression change. But he didn't hit her; he just turned away and walked out the door without saying goodbye.

She stood there, staring in confusion at the closed door. Then she felt cold, and went and peeked in the lukewarm stove. There was a pile of ashes in front of it from the morning. She should probably go to bed, but there was still straightening up to do. Why did her father get angry so suddenly? Hopefully her mother would come home soon.

She bent down and pushed the costume scraps into a pile with one hand. She could get a broom from the kitchen and sweep them up, but she never liked making a noise when she was home alone. She added the pile to the ashes, then she crouched down and looked at it. She reached out her hand, picked up a curl that had been cut off the wig, and pressed it between her fingers. It stung like nettle but she grasped it even tighter.

This must be made of glass, she thought, feeling something warm running down her cheeks. It was silly to cry over something like that.

She knew beforehand it would hurt.

One Morning in a Residential Neighborhood

It was fall, but the little girl insisted it was winter because she was cold, and she was wearing her new brown winter coat for the first time. Early that morning she had been woken by Hansen, even though her older brother was still sleeping. There was something unusual and exciting in the air, but she was so sleepy, she couldn't remember just then what was in store for her.

Hansen's voice was strangely slurred, and she was caressing every piece of clothing as if it were alive before she put it on the girl. The girl became attentive and took a closer look at the person she had known her entire short life. 'Why are you crying?' she asked, surprised. But that made Hansen upset, and she mumbled something about having a cold, that's why her eyes were red. She hadn't been crying.

Suddenly the girl realized what day it was, and her round little face broke out in a smile and she started babbling, 'I'm going on a trip with Daddy, Hansen, you know that, right? Can I say goodbye to Ole? Are Mommy and Daddy up yet?' But Hansen just shushed her and gently reprimanded her, saying, 'Don't wake up Ole; Daddy is up, but Mommy is still asleep.'

Then she led the girl from the dark, warm nursery, where the air was sweet and thick with the sleep of little children.

The girl was wearing her birthday dress, and she wanted to see herself in the mirror. Her nanny lifted her up. 'There you go; you're the one who gets to go with Daddy,' she said. 'You can bet Ole is upset he's not going.' Out of the flat, shiny mirror, two curious, excited eyes stared out at the child's own, but behind them was an adult's damp, pale face, and the child suddenly threw her arms around her nanny's neck. 'When am I coming back home?' she asked. There was a sudden touch of anxiousness in her voice. Hansen didn't answer, but set her carefully back down on the floor and started brushing the girl's long blonde hair with a slightly trembling hand. A little later she was able to say, 'It won't be so very long,' in a voice that she thought would be reassuring. Then she remembered the mother's numerous house rules. One of them was: You always have to tell a child the truth. She would rather be skinned alive than tell the truth at that moment. A wave of anger swept through her toward the mother of the child she loved more than any of the children she had ever known before in her life. They share children between them as if they were furniture, she thought, and when she heard the father's heavy steps upstairs: That poor man; she is destroying his world right now. She forgot about her self-effacing tenderness for the wife when she was sick and the children had to be kept away from her; and when she was healthy and sang during her morning shower, carefree and youthful; and the *thing* behind all of it. That kind of person, she thought vaguely, but got no further, before sorrow ambushed her again. Her tears dropped soundlessly into the girl's hair, glowing like a radiant halo around her precious little face.

The father came down the stairs, and she could see right away that he hadn't had enough sleep. He had dark circles under his eyes, and the young nanny didn't dare meet his gaze. She walked out to the kitchen to make coffee, and the child ran to her father, who picked her up in his arms and tried to smile. 'So, Kirsten, are you going on a trip with Daddy?' She was like a living ball of joy as she jumped down, then started running up the stairs, because everything wouldn't be so wonderful if her Mommy wasn't part of it. Her father tried to stop her, saying quietly, just like Hansen, 'Mommy is still sleeping.' He stood at the base of the stairs, combing his fingers through his hair, perplexed, while the child ran into her mother's bedroom, where it smelled soothingly of perfume, night, and mother. When she crawled in next to the warm, comforting body, her face got wet, and the delicate, vague anxiety returned for a moment. She said, 'Why are you crying, Mommy? I'll come back.' Her mother didn't answer, but pulled the little girl closer. They lay together like that, silently: the child confused and impatient, and the mother so distraught by grief and shame that her entire body was trembling like a sapling in a storm. Trembling, but motionless. Between her and the child was an invisible being, an unmerciful power. In a few hours, two strong arms would substitute for the child's tender, pure embrace. A lover's voice would comfort and explain. The fine autumn air in the yard, the flowers' aroma, and the long, happy days would temper the loss, and she knew it, and it made her feel weak and fallible: Dear God, she prayed, let this parting be the last one in my life.

The jumpy little body wriggled itself from her arms. The child wanted to envelop her with her happiness, and she tried to pull her mother out of bed, as she had done so many times before, so everything would be okay. 'Get up now, Mommy,' she shouted. 'You have to see the moving van. You have to wave goodbye to us. I'm going to put on my new coat – it's winter, Mommy. Do you remember when it was winter, and you went sledding with me and Daddy and Ole?'

She stayed upstairs while her mother dressed. The aroma of coffee rose to the bedroom, and with it a restlessness. The girl's brother was awake. Soon he would come running to say good morning, and probably be crabby because he wasn't going with his daddy. Daddy had found work in another city! Children are so willing to be tricked to avoid the truth they don't want to hear.

The little girl remained standing there mercilessly, while her mother did her hair at the vanity. Soon the movers would come tramping in, and carry down the furniture he wanted to take. She had begged him to take everything, to stay in the house and chase her out, if only she could keep both children. Fathers always forget their children when they haven't seen them for a long time. But what did she really know about that? If she had been more confident, she could have invoked the law, which rarely separates a child from its mother. But she wasn't certain about anything anymore, and she wasn't used to making big decisions on her own. Two different men wanted her to make this sacrifice. 'You can't take everything from him.' She owed it to two men. But a person doesn't sacrifice a child, do they? Well, she was doing it. Only her. It was her fault, and the most innocent of all people would pay for it. Here in this room, with the child beside her, she felt completely alone. Even the furniture seemed to shrink from her. Everything she knew was receding into a fog. If only it all could go back to how it was before! But nothing is ever the way it was. Life is change: passion, indifference, death. She was afraid of her child, afraid of all the life awaiting her downstairs: Miss Hansen's tearful, shaming, uncomprehending eyes; Ole's questions; and her husband's pained face. Oh God, this child! If only she had been a bit younger or a bit older. The people we love, she thought, as she put makeup on her pale face. What can I say? How can I stop it? My love, come and help me. Maybe it's too late for you to come. The pain of this morning will always be mine and mine alone. You will feel jealous if I even mention it. But all of us are alone. We three adults have been living here together in this house all these years. We love the children and they love us, and now we have to lie to them. How can I live a virtuous life when the footsteps and voice of a man can turn my heart away from everything that once gave me comfort? Why did I get married? Why did I have children? There is nothing so merciless as love.

Her eyes met the child's observant ones in the mirror, and she smiled at her. The girl jumped up on her mother's lap and put her warm cheek against her mother's. 'Mommy, today you have to eat breakfast with us, okay?' she said ingratiatingly, using the fine little voice she used – the one she had used quite often lately – when she wanted to chase away unpleasantness between the grown-ups.

Carrying her daughter she went downstairs, where the table was set for all of them. Otherwise the children usually ate by themselves. Her husband sat in his usual spot, and she immediately made the same observation as the nanny: He didn't sleep last night! She felt bad for him, as we do for people we have harmed. He sat there with his grief and hurt wrapped around him like a frayed jacket for everyone to see and feel sorry for. And here I come with my sacrifice, she thought; and to bear it, she had to imagine the face of her lover in front of her like an invisible shield. But the three pairs of eyes, which were turned mutely toward her, made her waver. She despised herself: Is all of life like an opera? She wanted to sing: Goodbye, goodbye, now I'm leaving and I'm taking someone else instead of you.

She sat down, defiant and erect at the table end, smiling bravely at her children. But she didn't dare look at Miss Hansen. Why did she arrange this comical farce, she thought angrily. All that's missing is lit candles on the table. Her son was grumpy and sleepy, as she had predicted. Suddenly she gave him an icy look, as if he had nothing to do with her, while she pushed in the chair under her daughter and tied the bib around her neck. For a moment it all seemed to her like a long, drawn-out sentimental scene from an American film, constructed so pitifully that people react by bursting out laughing: The sweet children, the wronged father, the loyal maid, and the flighty mother. What did all these people have to do with her? Why were they taking advantage of her love for this child? Only one single person really mattered to her, and he wasn't here. But his shadow suffused her expression like a flimsy defense against something horrible. And beyond him: millions of miserable children, tons of loyal housekeepers and an incalculable army of lovers, abandoned husbands, disloyal husbands, betrayed and flighty women, all kinds of people, all kinds of lives, and all equally lonely. And overshadowing everything: some kind of law, war, profound misery, making a living, fear of the newspapers' bold headlines, a world in tension, and hopelessly patient, calm. A whip is raised over all of us; where and whom will it hit?

She ate her egg in silence, letting the nanny take care of the children. She still had not met her husband's gaze. You have to do it, her lover had said. Time is of the essence. If you keep on being weak and yielding, life will pass you by. Try to see it from a broader perspective.

But soon the moving van would be there, and it was up to them to make it a celebratory event for the girl. They had agreed on that. She pulled herself together and was about to say something, when Ole, who was going to turn eight soon, suddenly looked around strangely from one to the other and asked, 'So when is Kirsten coming back home?'

No one was able to answer. As soon as the girl was out of the house, she would have to explain to him how things were. He was old enough to understand, and it was important that he also believed something new and exciting was in store for him.

All at once she felt so terribly tired, hating the nanny, who sniffled loudly, hating all of them because they didn't understand her, and hating herself most of all because she didn't know if she was doing the right thing. She felt a sudden, crushing desire to sob in her lover's arms. Her tears were stuck, burning behind her dry eyes. How did a five-year-old child comprehend this? When would she feel betrayed, and how would the truth come out?

Finally the moving van arrived, red and boisterous and festive, and the children ran out to the road to catch sight of the men who would carry so much away. The nanny got up and ran to her room, and the two of them were alone for a moment. They had nothing to say to one another, but a strange feeling of mutual pain was in their eyes when they eventually met. He blinked a few times like a young boy, and she saw something in his expression that she had once loved.

It wasn't possible for him to hate her. For some reason he had become used to not blaming her for her actions. He was indifferent about his own life; he was only consumed with the thought that he didn't want to die. A person doesn't die when he has a child to take care of and protect. Besides, she could see the girl once in a while, if she wanted to, and he wanted to see his son. But at this moment he felt the same mild indifference for himself that she did. It was as if they only had this one child together. He had fertilized her back then, and now he was taking the child with him. She had to pay. But she would forget soon enough. When a woman is in love–

For twenty minutes there was noise and activity throughout the house, and then the girl was sitting next to the driver in her fine brown coat with a velvet cap over her blonde curls. She looked at her mother with a slightly anxious expression, and she put her arms around her one last time and whispered to comfort her, 'When it's summer I'll come back, okay?'

Her mother nodded and smiled and waved, as long as she could see the van. Then the smile faded from her face, as if a hard hand had wiped it off. She took the boy by the hand and started walking slowly back to the house.

A Nice Boy

The forest warden's son squeezed between the other customers in the bakery shop. He stood on his toes to be seen, and he kept a close eye on who came in after him. He was in a hurry. He almost always was. He needed a bottle of milk for his little brother. His mother was suddenly unable to nurse him anymore, because she had a tumor in her breast, and a fever.

He craned his neck trying to catch the eye of the baker, who was really taking his time. The mother of one of his classmates came into the store, and he quickly removed his hat, like a recruit to an officer. 'Hello,' he said.

She was grappling with a shopping bag in front of her, from which the ends of leeks stuck out and tickled his neck.

'Hello, John. Congratulations on your new little brother. Isn't it wonderful?'

'Yep,' he said, blushing bright red in his effort to express overwhelming joy.

They all turned to stare at him. Was he really happy?

'No one was expecting that, were they?' said the baker, smiling at a customer. 'Got it in just under the wire.'

Then he turned to the boy.

'And what do you need today?'

John lifted his basket up onto the counter and handed him the note his mother had written. 'Otherwise you'll forget half of it,' she had said. He had never forgotten anything yet, but she always said things like that. He took the filled basket from the baker, with the change wrapped in the note.

'Is he a cute little one?' asked the baker, stroking his beard.

The boy nodded. 'I guess,' he said, 'but he screams a lot.'

They all laughed, like adults always do when you don't just say 'yes' or 'no'. He thought he saw them looking at one another and winking as he hurried out the door.

Outside, the cold greeted him and made him sneeze. The woods rose like a huge mountain in front of him, and the house at the bottom was like a tiny dot. If he ran across the fields, he could be home in fifteen minutes; on the road it took half an hour. But it was too light out to trespass.

The basket was heavy, so he switched it to his other arm and continued at a half-run. He wanted to surprise his mother by coming back lightning-fast, which he always did. But today he wanted it to be even faster, because she was sick and his little brother needed the milk right away. Cars streamed past him, but he couldn't see the license plates, which he otherwise kept track of, because of the snowflakes. A few cyclists struggled by, bent over their handlebars, with earmuffs and damp, red faces. But the ones coming toward him had the wind at their backs, and he recognized all of them. 'Hi John!' they shouted. He nodded enthusiastically. No one could say he was impolite. He was the nicest boy in the whole area when it came to running errands, chopping wood, washing diapers, and whatever else a person has to do to get ahead in the world. The only thing that didn't go so smoothly was his schoolwork. His mother said, 'Don't worry about that; as long as you're a nice boy.' His mother was so sweet, and so kind. He was a little scared of his father, who didn't talk to him very much. His father's voice was coarse and hard, just like his hands when he slung the rifle down from his shoulder and tossed a dead squirrel on the kitchen counter. They were harmful animals, and he got money from the estate owner for every one he shot. But they looked comical when they dashed up the tree trunks, always running away. John wished he could hold a live squirrel in his hands one day. They wouldn't have to be scared of him. He had only touched his father's rifle once, and he still remembered the spanking he got for it. 'It could go off,' his mother had explained, 'and hit you or one of us.' What if it hit his little brother? Who knows what would happen? Then his mother and father would regret ever 'taking him in'.

He raced ahead at the thought. He knew he was in debt to humanity because he wasn't born properly to his mother and father like his little brother, but had ended up with them, by an improbable stroke of luck. He was adopted, and his real parents were horrible people from Copenhagen, who weren't even married. 'God forbid you ever meet them,' his mother had said when she told him that. For a while afterward he would stare at the outsiders who visited his town, imagining they had come from Copenhagen to take him away. He would put up such a fight and yell for his mother! He might be small for a seven-year-old, but he was strong. He could pump water from the well and carry two buckets at once. Little brother might never be able to do that. Such a runt. He lay at his mother's breast, sucking like crazy until it made her sick. One day John asked if *he* had ever eaten like that, and his mother laughed. 'No, you poor thing; you were bottle-fed.' He imagined that he might have been made in a bottle, just like people make ships in bottles, but now he knew what it meant. It just sounded so strange to be different. And he would always be different, but only in a good way. He could run faster than any boy in his class.

His breath steamed from his mouth like smoke from his father's pipe. He sniffled and switched the basket between his arms again. Then he paused to wipe his nose on his sleeve. Now the woods weren't like a mountain anymore, and he could see smoke rising from the chimney. He could also hear an axe chopping, which was his father, felling trees. The estate owner marked the victims himself. They just stood there not knowing anything until they felt the axe on their trunks. Until then, they were just like any other trees, figuring they would stand there for all time, blowing in the wind, sending out new shoots in the spring and losing it all when the cold arrived, making the poor squirrels visible from a distance. He felt bad for the trees, but his mother said trees didn't feel anything. The little squirrels didn't know they had to be shot either, and it didn't hurt them at all when their heart was struck by a pellet. Only poachers were bad, because they often didn't shoot right, and they let the animals lie there until his father found them. His father loved animals. They had three hunting dogs and a little fox terrier, which was going to be shot soon, because it shed, and all the dog hair made little brother cough. The doctor had said that. Still, John loved that dog.

The arrival of the baby had brought with it lots of other things. In the middle of the night the baby woke him with his screaming, and even when John broke his own record crossing the distance from the bakery or from school, sometimes his mother forgot to notice. In his disappointment he pointed it out to her himself. 'I made it in only ten minutes today, Mommy –' and she looked briefly in his direction and exclaimed, 'You are incredible. You are the best ever. What would we ever do without you?' But it wasn't as big a deal as it used to be.

Without thinking about it, the boy slowed down in the final stretch. The milk was sloshing in the bottle. 'It is amazing how much the little tyke can get down,' said his mother, with the baby at her bosom. But in a different tone of voice than when they said (and it was mostly his father): 'The way he puts it away he'll eat us out of house and home.' Then it was John they meant. And the food caught in his throat, while his cheeks turned bright red. Then his mother laughed and patted his head. 'If only all that eating would make him taller,' she said kindly. So his father hadn't meant anything mean by it. But still!

He jumped up a snowbank at the road edge, slid down the other side, and looked up at the next one. He laughed at his little game, and forgot he was in a hurry. His mother was home in bed, sick because of the baby, and his father would come home soon from the woods and make dinner, while John set the table. It felt strange to eat alone with him. When he was in a good mood, he teased the boy. 'So Mister Front Teeth,' he said, 'how was your day?' John had lost his two front teeth, and the father insisted they wouldn't grow back. 'That's nonsense,' said his mother, annoyed. 'The boy could go and think it was true!' His dear mother – so fat, so warm, so good.

He started running again for the last little bit, past the pump that looked like an old man with a cold, with clothes draped all over it so it wouldn't freeze; past a load of firewood standing in the farmyard, waiting for its turn in the stove. He had helped to stack it during the summer. He had pretended the pieces of wood were soldiers, and really he wanted to stand them up vertically in ranks, but that took up too much space. Work was his play and play his work. And that was perfectly fine, until his little brother was born. Then the wet diapers became pirate flags, but he was a tired little pirate who had too many enemies to overcome. And the baby was a prince, who was going to inherit a kingdom one day. John was his slave, whom he always sought for advice in difficult situations. 'Ask my slave,' he would say. 'He brought me up, so he gets to decide everything.'

John lifted the door latch and stepped into the

kitchen. Then he put the basket on the stove and stood there listening. There was a voice coming from the living room in addition to his mother's. They didn't hear him come in. He could hear it was their neighbor, Mrs Petersen, who often came by to have a cup of coffee.

'Well, aren't you thrilled that you were finally able to?' To what? It wasn't nice to eavesdrop, but it sounded so interesting.

'Do you really have to ask, after all these years?'

'If only you had known when you took in John!' It sounded like a complaint, and John stiffened at hearing his own name.

'Well,' his mother said hesitantly, 'we've never been sorry about that for a moment. He is such a nice and capable boy.'

'He certainly has been a big help to you.'

There was something about the tone that made a little pain gnaw deep into John.

'Well, Mrs Petersen, it's no trouble for him. He's never happier than when he can help us with something.' Now his mother sounded upset, and John wanted to run in there and support her. But he wanted to hear himself praised a bit more too.

'No, of course,' said the other woman effusively. 'And God knows where the poor child would have been without you. It was such a good deed you did. Is he thankful? Because he knows, doesn't he?'

'He is definitely thankful,' said his mother, and out by the kitchen door John stood thankfully and in solidarity with her. 'And of course we have told him. A child finds out those kinds of things sooner or later, and my husband also thought it was for the best.'

He pulled off his mittens and stopped listening. His heart was pounding. He hadn't run fast enough; he wasn't thankful enough. He wasn't like other children. He was 'taken in'. Inside him, a bad conscience started growing like a heavy, thick substance. He wanted to light the stove before his father got home. He wanted to get the bottle ready for his little brother and make a scrambled egg with sugar for his mother. He wanted to get up tonight when the baby cried, so his mother could stay asleep, he wanted–

'Well, God Almighty, are you standing there, John?'

Mrs Petersen tied her kerchief around her head and stared at him dubiously. Had he heard anything? He wasn't as adorable as the little one in there, she concluded. You never really warm up to children like that, but he did work like a horse all day long while other children were playing. Everyone talked about this and acted as if they found it troubling, but deep inside they all thought it was perfectly fine.

The boy bowed his head, afraid she was going to take his hand. Her hands were so limp and always smelled like dishwater or something else repulsive. They reminded him of the dead animals on the kitchen counter that his father got money for killing – squirrels and voles, and sometimes a small deer with gentle, stiffened eyes and legs sticking out, like it couldn't get over the surprise that suddenly everything was gone forever. To get shot is like falling asleep, his mother said, who used to feel bad for all the little creatures herself.

Mrs Petersen left, and the boy hurried into the living room. His mother lay on the sofa looking exhausted, with her eyes closed. The baby was sleeping in the cradle by the wood stove.

'Wasn't I fast?' he asked carefully.

Slowly she opened her eyes.

'Oh, it's you,' she said. 'You are such a good boy.' Then she dozed off again. The boy heard the clunk of his father outside, taking off his clogs, and the dogs barking and rushing at the door.

He stood there looking at his mother lying with her mouth open. He wanted to be even better and run even faster. He knew he owed a debt to these people, which he paid off in little installments and with his meager abilities. If only I was big, he thought, growing sleepy from the warmth in the room. Feeling uneasy, he snuck past his father in the little entry and out to the kitchen. His father didn't greet him, perhaps didn't even notice him.

'How is the little one?' he shouted.

'Shhh,' whispered his mother gently. 'He's sleeping.'

Then the boy started to light the stove. The cold iron rings stung like fire against his numbed hands.

Life's Persistence

The waiting room was filled with women who avoided looking at one another. They looked down at the dusty floor, at the tips of their shoes, at the dirty wall of undefinable color. (Why is it that these doctors who earn so much money always have such shabby offices? Maybe he won't even wear a lab coat and he probably has dirty fingernails.) They were all so discreet and dressed so self-effacingly, they could slip in anywhere without anyone noticing them. Maybe they had received the same advice she had: *He determines the price based on your clothing.* Besides, the other women were no business of hers. Couldn't she drop her habit of concerning herself with everyone and everything around her, just this once? No. She couldn't bring the seriousness of the situation into focus. Was it all that serious after all? In any case it wasn't any worse for her than for the others. Behind each of these women was the shadow of a man: a tired husband who toiled for a throng of children, and whose income couldn't bear the strain of another child; a disloyal chap with pomaded hair who was already a thing of the past, an ephemeral, hasty tryst that had little to do with love; a student who was loved but too young, who was now pacing outside on the sidewalk, teetering between hope and fear; a carefree, superficial guy who had 'found an address' and bought a way out of the predicament he had gotten himself into; or one who had moved away from the city and left his difficult burden here like a piece of forgotten furniture; at any rate a man, a trap, a careless, costly experience, maybe the first one–

There was no rush to get inside the closed door, which every now and then was opened from the inside by a young woman, who, quickly and without looking at anyone, left the sad waiting room, relieved or not, to slip back into the afternoon's noisy rush-hour traffic, down below on the other side of the murky windows.

It was so quiet. Alice thought about Bent. There was something clearly laughable about the thought of having a child with him, and not the least heroic in hiding it from him. A child? A little wrinkled thing under powder-blue ruffles, staring out at the world with the unknowing intelligent gaze of an infant. A bond between two who loved one another; but their love couldn't bear a bond like that. They agreed on that from the beginning. He was burdened enough by a wife who let him do whatever he wanted, as long as she and their child were supported and the outer appearance of civility and domesticity was maintained. Why should Alice come and disrupt that calm? She looked at her relationship to Bent with cool reason. He was only loving if she kept it easy and ephemeral. In that way she had extended it to nearly a year, and when they hadn't had any accidents, they had become careless. It was mostly her fault. A person doesn't go around thinking they will break their leg every time they cross the street. And anyway she wasn't going to reproach others for something that happened to her. And if it were the man's body that had to go through this, she knew that Bent would never have complained to her about it, just as he barely complained to her about his marriage tedium, which naturally was not as tedious as the way he expressed it to her, albeit tactfully. When he came home from work, their child jumped up to greet him, and he picked it up in his arms and they played together. Then he kissed his wife and was happy about her pretty, domestic appearance, the finely set table, the aromas emanating from the kitchen, and his desk, which alone bore the mark of his disorganized habits and his quick-witted mind with its clear, cool, reasoning intellect, which she loved about him. But all of this was conjecture on her part. He never talked about it, and she wasn't curious. She abhorred the usual: My wife doesn't understand me, etc. She had patiently shared him with this strange woman whom she had never seen. Don't demand much, and you'll get more. And if she just caressed his forehead, the memory of his life apart from hers was gone for several hours. This is how she held onto his love, and he didn't harm either of them. *Neither of us,* she stated clearly in her mind. For some reason it was important to recognize that.

She turned her gaze somewhat uneasily toward the closed door and felt a little dispirited. A distasteful undertaking, she thought. Nothing to do with murder or 'the sanctity of motherhood' – phrases she had had plenty of from the proper law-abiding doctors in proper lab coats behind proper desks. She was twenty-five years old and master of her own body, not according to the law, which she could not care less about, but because she *wanted* to be. Not a single sentimental thought about powder-blue ruffles and a little toothless grin. There were already plenty of babies in the world. And this little parasite had only brought her nausea and discomfort, and left a slimy, gray veil over everything that used to be nice: the first rays of morning under the roll-down shades; the coffee she had to switch to tea, which didn't taste good to her anymore either; the evening's heart-wrenching yearning for Bent, which had changed into yawning exhaustion, difficult to keep hidden for long. Besides, recently he had only come by a couple of times a week. That made sense. She wasn't too crazy about being with a man who just wanted to feel good and fall asleep in her arms. She remembered how agitated she was when he had a tooth abscess which made his cheek swell up, and they couldn't be seen out together. It fit as badly with his handsome, well-chiseled face as a grotesque swollen belly would fit with her hourglass waist, of which she was so proud. Everything oppressive about marriage had to be kept out of their relationship. Wouldn't it look fine if she called him up now and said in a tearful wifely voice: There's something we absolutely have to discuss right now! She wasn't the strongest person, for better or for worse. She wasn't going to try to convince him to leave his wife and child on account of this accident. She was afraid of hurting anyone, and she had the innate conviction that love and marriage rarely had anything to do with one another.

Her turn was approaching soon; in her mind she repeated her false name and her 'desperate circumstances'. He would ask, 'Why can't you keep the baby?', spuriously and pro forma. She already couldn't stand him, the way you might feel antipathy toward a stranger on whose mercy you depend. Naturally she should – well, what should she do? She knew herself. She was no proud, heroic character who could be a 'self-supporting, single mother' and disregard the prejudices of others. Maybe single and self-supporting, but not mother. Not this way, in any case. A ball and chain to a man – an obligation! She had always imagined that someday they would part with neither tears nor regrets, something like: Thank you for the time we have spent together. But later, much later, as much later as possible. Evenings without him? The city lights and fun without him?

She stood up in her stained cotton coat, nauseous and uneasy and – and something else she didn't have a name for, which was hers alone. But didn't she leave him alone with his tooth abscess? Hot compresses, and, for that matter, also pregnancy, belong to marriage, and if she wasn't going to have its pleasantries, then she didn't want to be bothered with its difficulties. Even though Bent had never talked about it, she could tell he was fond of his child, that he was a fine father and husband. It was simply a side of him which had nothing to do with her (but which she was definitely helping to maintain). With a tiny dash of bitterness, she thought about how nice it must be to return to a well-ordered home after the embraces of a lover.

'Next!'

Spindly and erect, with dark circles under her eyes, she walked reluctantly into the dimly lit room. Her heart, which should have been rational and hard, was hammering with anxiety and defiance.

He barely looked at her. He was sitting at a desk, half in shadow, without a lab coat, as she had imagined. He lazily gestured with his hand toward an empty chair. Her lips were dry, and for a few minutes neither of them said anything. The man stared out the window while he drummed on the desktop with a pencil. His dark eyebrows met in the middle, but Alice only saw his hands, which were large and hairy, and for that moment she was horrified at the thought that he was going to touch her.

When he was finished with his calculations, he suddenly tossed down the pencil and turned to face her. He bit vigorously into his bottom lip and finally asked:

'So what is the matter?'

She wet her lips with her tongue and cleared her throat.

'I – am going to have a baby,' she said quietly, adding, before thinking about it: 'You know that very well.'

'How should I know that?' he asked with voice like a scratchy record.

A helpless feeling came over Alice. She had been told that she should 'go about it carefully', and before she had come, it had all seemed so clear to her, so right and natural; but even the man's appearance and manner gave her a sense of shame, of something unclean and terrible. She didn't understand anything, herself least of all, when she answered:

'Isn't that what you do for a living?'

She had snubbed the lifeline the man had extended. She had done something irrevocable, something whose consequences she couldn't foresee. Her reason had abandoned her.

The man's expression was vacant and uncomprehending. Without looking at her, he took out a smudged handkerchief and started cleaning his eyeglasses very energetically.

'I don't understand at all what you mean,' he said flatly.

Then the words came out by themselves, as if they had always been somewhere in the world, waiting for her, as if the entire situation had been constructed and laid out in advance – perhaps as long as she had been alive – and little could be changed about it, as much as wishful thinking could change the weather tomorrow.

She straightened herself in the chair and smoothed out her dress, over her flat belly, which would soon start swelling unmercifully.

'I mean,' she said calmly, 'this is the first time, you

understand, and – and – don't I have to be examined or something?'

He rose with a gracefulness that one would never have thought possible of such a body, and it seemed to Alice that a kind of comic annoyance or impatience was evident in his movements, as he walked past her in the tiny room, where there stood a gurney.

'If you undress, I will examine you. Go right ahead.'

Her knees were shaking a little as she followed him, very erect and pale. She thought to herself, *I will often need to remember the triumph of this moment.*

Five minutes later they were sitting across from one another again. He looked at her askance over his glasses. A crooked smile quivered at the edge of his mouth. She put all the contempt she possibly could into her expression, but she couldn't make his smile go away.

Then he said slowly, with a slight, ironic bow in her direction:

'You are about three months along – congratulations, Madam.'

Then they both got up, and he reached out his hand. Childishly, she pretended not to see it as she opened her purse and took out her wallet. 'How much do I owe you?'

'Twenty kroner, please.'

He held the door open for her as she left the consultation room.

'Next!' he shouted.

Not until she was down on the street, where people brushed into her impatiently on their way home for dinner, did she feel like herself again, her horrified soul reeling for support like a drunkard. Something Bent had once said occurred to her: It's not our words that reveal our character, it's the deeds we undertake, regardless of their logic. What did his child look like? The thought had never occurred to her before. A pain she had never felt before was burrowing and burning inside her. The deeds we undertake–

Slowly, with her hands in her pockets and her shiny hair blowing in the wind, she walked home to her lonely rented room.

Evening

Hanne was only seven, but she already possessed a great deal of formless anxiety. She always wanted to be some-where other than where she was at that moment. When she sat in the nursery with her little brother, who was completely absorbed with playing, she would listen for her father's and mother's steps downstairs and do what she could to follow their strange conversation. They spoke differently with each other when they were alone than when she was listening. Her mother's voice went delicate and quiet, which made her own belly feel both nice and bad – mostly bad – and her father laughed at what her mother said almost all the time. If Hanne came jumping or sneaking down the stairs, they went completely quiet. Then her mother might say, 'How about going out to play, honey?' And if Hanne walked over to her, she didn't put her on her lap or tell her sto-ries, but went kind of stiff, so Hanne herself became nearly immobile, feeling her father's expression wrap a dark cloak of anxiety around both of them. Then her mother said, without looking at her, 'How about going back up and playing with your little brother? Your dad-dy's tired.' But that wasn't true at all, because he could just go to bed and sleep, like other people did when

85

they were tired, and he wasn't even the one who said it. He never said much to Hanne, and when he did, he just asked what two times twenty was, or if she had learned to read yet, but he didn't always listen to how she answered.

Still, he was a nice daddy, because he had never hit her or yelled at her at all, and she knew he went to work every day to earn money for clothes and food for all of them, and it would be the most horrible thing if he left them. Her mother had explained this to her one day when Hanne suddenly said, 'Oh, Daddy is so stupid', when she saw him turn in through the garden gate on his bicycle, just as they were having such a cozy time, she and her Mommy.

There was so much to be afraid of and to be careful about. First and foremost, she had to watch her little brother, who could get strangled in his baby carriage harness or who could grab a few matches and set himself or the whole house on fire. Hanne could never relax except when she was sleeping at night, when she was relieved of her anxiousness. Not because she would be so heartbroken if her little brother died, but her mother would be so terribly sad and she would cry for days and days, just like back when Hanne's real father left them, and everything was so cheerless until they got a new one.

When they had guests, her mother laughed while she told the story of Hanne running up to window cleaners and different men she saw to ask them if they would marry her mother. Hanne didn't think it was funny, because without a daddy in the house, they would die of hunger. And she had no interest in dying and going down in the ground with no blanket over her at night. Evidently you turned into an angel and could fly up to God, but what if he came too late with your wings because there were too many others who died just at that moment, and he had to take care of all of them himself, just like her mother, since now they didn't have enough money for a nanny?

Her little brother was sleeping, and Hanne lay scratching the paint off her bed's blue rails. She never fell asleep before she heard her mother and father go to bed, and sometimes not until they had stopped talking in their bedroom and she was sure they were sleeping, so nothing could change during the course of the night.

They were still talking, down in the living room. Their quiet alone-voices, with her father's laughter and long pauses in between, made her head hurt, like when her little brother dumped all his blocks down on the floor at once. Maybe they were kissing one another, because that was part of being married, but not when the children are looking, because it's not good for them. 'Wait until we're alone,' her mother said once. 'It would be a sin for the child to see us.' Why would it be a sin? Sin had something to do with God and bedtime prayers.

Hanne lay down on her back and folded her hands on top of the comforter. Then God was in the room, but you couldn't see him, even if you turned on the light. Hanne imagined that he looked like her real father, who

was the biggest and strongest man in the whole world.
She closed her eyes and whispered the best of all bedtime prayers:

> Now I lay down in my bed
> close my eyes and bow my head
> Dear Lord, please look down with grace
> upon our shabby rented place.

Then she sighed, sleepy and serene, until her thoughts
came streaming back like hungry birds to a spring
garden bed.

If only they would come upstairs soon. Hanne's eyes
were starting to smart. The day after tomorrow was
Sunday, and she was going to visit her real father and
his new wife, who was much prettier than her mother,
but still repulsive. Goodness knows her father didn't
really love her, because they didn't have any children,
and people only had children if they loved each other
very much, like her mother loved her new father, back
when she had her little brother. But luckily that passed,
because after that there were no more babies who
could be strangled by their harnesses or who could set
the house on fire. Loving someone couldn't be helped.
It came and went like whooping cough. But it was no
use if only one person was the loving one, and that was
a good thing, because Hanne loved her math teacher
and her real father and her mother of course, and of
the three she was only certain that her father loved
her back. And she couldn't marry her father since he
was old, like she would be when she grew up and got

breasts and things like that, and you couldn't get married before then. If only she had been just as big as her father's new wife, whom she was supposed to call Grete-mom, when she stayed with them. But her father just called her Grete. Boy, was she dumb. And she had so many fancy dresses, a lot more than her mother. 'Don't worry about that,' her mother said. 'Only dumb people concern themselves with dressing up all the time.' But that her father, who was so smart, liked to kiss and be nice to such a dummy! Even though she had those long curls and eyes that always looked damp, as if she had just been crying. And she always laughed at everything, even when Hanne misbehaved. Last time she was there, Grete had put on a long silk gown with nothing on top, and spun around in front of Hanne and said, 'Don't you think I look pretty?' And Hanne had borrowed a joke from her limited, newly acquired vocabulary from school: 'Yes! From behind and in the dark!' But then they had both laughed so much that Hanne ended up crying and had to be comforted on her father's lap like a little baby, and she drew out her crying until Grete-mom stopped laughing. Served her right!

Hanne sniffled and pulled her handkerchief out from under her pillow. She blew her nose and rubbed it afterward, which she wasn't supposed to do, because then her nostrils would get big and open and the rain would go right in them. 'I don't care,' she said aloud, like when she hurt herself and didn't cry. She meant it about a lot of things. There were lots of things you could say 'I don't care' about. About Grete-mom, about if little brother got strangled, about her new father who mustn't leave them, about if he did leave, about if they got a new one–

Suddenly she sat up in bed with her heart pounding. There was a new voice in the living room. A loud, happy, loving and familiar voice, which sounded just the same whether you were there or not. But it couldn't be. Why would he come here? She listened. It was really *him*. He had come to chase out the new father and marry her mother again. Grete-mom must have died. Then her mother would get all her pretty dresses. She jumped out of bed and pulled up on her nightgown and raced down the stairs. 'Daddy!' she shouted, seeing nothing but him as, blinded by the light, she ran right into his tall body and let herself be enveloped in his familiar smell and touch in a blessed, all-shielding embrace. Then she blinked her eyes and looked at her father and mother who slowly solidified into two stiff, distant figures outside her world.

'Your daddy wants you to go with him now,' said her mother with a slight unfamiliar quaver in her voice. 'Go upstairs and get dressed, Hanne, but be careful not to wake up your little brother.'

There were three coffee cups on the table, and the living room seemed smaller than usual.

Her father straightened up, still with one hand on the girl's neck. She bored a finger into one of his button-holes and spun it around. Her whole body felt warm, as if she had just been in a bath.

'Aren't you going to stay here, Daddy?' she whispered anxiously, staring up into his big bright eyes.

Then her new father stood up and violently pushed in his chair.

'Couldn't this have waited until tomorrow?' he said in a thin, sharp voice. 'Who tears a child out of bed at this time of night?'

Her father didn't answer, but bent down again and pulled her close. 'Wouldn't you like to go on a trip with Grete-mom and me?' he asked. 'She's out in the car.'

Then Hanne went as stiff as her mother. 'Isn't she dead?' she asked, her mouth going dry.

'But Hanne, dear,' said her mother. 'Don't talk like that. You don't have to go if you don't want to.' And her father released her suddenly, as if he had burned himself. For a moment he stood there alone, not knowing what to do with his hands or his eyes. Then her new father took her hand and started leading her up the stairs, while the silence behind them hurt just as much as his hard, unfamiliar grasp. She didn't want to cry before she was in bed. No, she wasn't going to cry; she wasn't even going to bed. She was going on a trip and she was going to sit on her father's lap the whole way.

'Let me go!' she yelled, twisting her hand out of the man's grip and running back into the sharp light, where her mother sat, looking pitiful, and where there was a father too many. Something unmerciful, a totally new anxiety, kept her from seeking the most comforting shelter she knew. She stood hanging her head in front of her father, who had put on his hat, as if his work here was finished. She felt cold and shrugged her spindly shoulders and stepped hard on her own toes, as she gazed helplessly and imploringly at her mother, who was looking up at the man on the stairway with an anxious, pleading expression, as if it were she who had said something wrong.

He walked down the stairs with hard, deliberate steps. 'Let's get this over with right now,' he said tersely. 'Are you coming or not, Hanne?'

She looked down at her father's feet. Her forehead was burning with confusion, shame, and defiance. She took the difficult steps toward him, but he didn't touch her. His clothes smelled of distant, lost things. The whole way she could sit and sleep with her nose buried in his smell with her back to Grete-mom.

'I – want to come,' she begged, humbled with defeat.

When the girl went upstairs to get dressed, three people watched her lonely little figure. None of them could help her, and they didn't dare look at one another.

Depression

Lulu stacked the dirty dishes on top of one another in the nearly scalding water, so parsley sprigs, wilted lettuce leaves, and radish tops released and floated on top in a sad, greasy stew, which she appraised, disgusted for a moment, before she could bring herself to plunge her hands down into it and bring the porcelain back out. First the plates, then the forks, knives, and glasses. She used a lot of water. Behind her, the dented kettle was boiling dry, because she kept forgetting to fill it.

She heard noise and laughter from the living room. It was a festive, successful evening, and she knew it made a little dip in the mood when she, the hostess, in the middle of all the merriment, broke away to do the dishes. But she couldn't face waking up in the morning to a messy kitchen. Kai would just have to figure it out. She could hear his voice among the others; he spoke quickly, nervously, excitedly. He drank and smoked like crazy, and forgot to be accommodating to the guests when she wasn't around.

It would be so wonderful if his depression were over and done with. It had lasted from the moment they realized she was definitely pregnant for the second time in their marriage. The first depression lasted until she was five months along. And now little Bent was only one and a half. Of course it was unfortunate, but to her mind it wasn't the end of the world. And certainly not for him. In the end, she was the one who had to do the heavy lifting. But she was, as Kai put it, so healthy and well-adjusted. The nausea, the exhaustion, and everything that came with it, she knew would come to an end shortly. The economic stress would have to be borne by Kai (or more correctly, his parents), and unlike her complaints, that would only increase after the baby was born.

His studies would be finished in a year. But he had done no work for the last three months; he just lay all day long on the divan without sleeping or doing anything. If she tiptoed through the living room, he gave her a pained, unhappy look, which made her feel guilty, because she never knew if she should lie down beside him and caress his forehead, or if that would just bother him.

He went to psychoanalysis, but she didn't think it was helping. On the contrary, it cost a fortune, and this stranger (his analyst), whom she had never seen, instilled in her a distrust and something resembling jealousy. He had suggested admittance to an institution, but Kai didn't want that, because of his parents, who lived at their parsonage in Jylland and supported them, and who mustn't at any cost be upset by bad news from Copenhagen. He was their only child, and they expected a result from investing in their son in the form of a newly hatched doctor.

Every time he had gone to psychoanalysis, Kai showed animosity toward her and Bent afterward, and he was more irritable than usual. If she didn't know better, she would think he had returned from being with another woman. Sometimes she wished it were something like that. At least that was something you could wrap your head around, a battle you could win or lose. The way it was now, it was like some strong, invisible enemy was sapping her energy, but she wasn't supposed to feel that way. Sometimes Kai tried to discuss it with her. 'It's important that one person in the world totally understands why I react the way I do,' he explained.

During his first depression, Kai had begun studying 'mental mechanisms' and things like that; and when he started to brighten up again, he would only spend time with people who were involved in similar pursuits. They were studying for a test (she didn't know what the subject was) or had already taken it. They often (no, almost exclusively) spoke with tortured faces about the doctors' distrust of them, and they challenged Kai to 'do something for their cause' in his medical capacity. She had the vague feeling that they were in the process of seducing him into something mystical of which she could never be a part, since she, according to their 'teaching', could never understand or help him, because she was too close. But when his mood changed, and suddenly he wanted to have people around him, he gushed with brightness and attentiveness. 'You have been so amazing,' he said then. 'How would I have ever gotten through this without you?'

Lulu sat down for a minute on the kitchen counter and wearily brushed her hair back from her forehead with her hand. Kai's voice reached her from the living room: 'The essential difference between a depression and a neurosis . . .'

She jumped down and started putting things away, rattling them unnecessarily loudly. They always talked like that. Psychoanalysis, repression, hypnosis, depression, neurosis, mania! Sometimes she actually felt guilty over her own boring psyche, and found herself rather lacking, that in the middle of a crazy and besieged world she could keep her grip on the insignificant, necessary things which formed the foundation of their existence. But she was incurably normal, even though Kai asserted at times that she was full of inhibitions and complexes which she wouldn't acknowledge. 'The way the world looks today,' he said, 'it's more a wonder that a person can keep their ego together, than that they give up.' He looked at her with a cool, questioning face, as if she were a kitten playing in the middle of a pile of smoldering ruins. She wondered how he would take it if one day she 'gave up'!

Lulu removed her apron and walked to the bathroom to straighten her appearance a bit before returning to their guests. God knows if they would be gone by midnight. Kai slept so poorly, despite the sleeping pills and sedatives; but for the time being it didn't matter that he wasn't sleeping. He woke her early in the morning and was innocent, happy, and full of pep, kissing her lovingly and playing with Bent and laying out the wildest plans for the future. She had become used to hearing about them, and she listened in the same way that she listened to the child's excited, awkward babbling. They would have their own house, or a farm with blue shutters and a thatched roof, a puppy at least – people could learn a lot from animals: give them neuroses, create conditioned reflexes, etc. Anyway it was wrong the way they walled themselves in and never saw other people. It wasn't healthy for her either–

He was like that this morning, and he had called far and wide to invite people over. All day he had helped her prepare for the party. Everything was bought on credit; everything always got paid for at the last possible moment. She had to take detours so she wouldn't pass the stores where they were in debt. Owing money didn't bother Kai, who was otherwise so picky about things. But it bothered her enormously. Inviting people over and filling them with food and wine that hadn't been paid for took away half the enjoyment for her. But she had been happy most of the day, because Kai was. He opened cans, brought the wine to room temperature, and gave her advice with regards to spices and vegetables that would liven up the table.

In the midst of all their preparations, Kai sat down with Bent on his lap, testing the boy in various ways to display his intelligence. Bent was in good form today, and the child was jubilant when he guessed right. 'Daddy happy!' he shouted, and Kai was moved and thoughtful a moment, as he set the child down in the playpen. 'It's a shame it affects other people when you feel a certain way,' he said. In her hands, tenderly, she had taken his fine, narrow face, which already bore the indelible mark of his secret inner pain, from which she couldn't relieve him. 'A day like today offsets this whole, long, difficult period for all of us,' she said softly.

But it was so hard to stay on his wavelength for an

extended period. He pulled a book down from the shelf and read aloud to her – one of his study books, replete with red underlining – while she stood over a pan of scrambled eggs. She could detect in his voice when she should smile or nod understandingly. She felt like an idiot. The words didn't really reach her; she just listened for the excitement and intensity in his voice, and she thought about a thousand other things at the same time: How was she going to seat nine people at the dining table? They were short two glasses, and one was chipped, but she could use that one. With some goodwill, three people could sit on the divan.

Kai approached the boy again – something about drawings from the book he wanted to try. An ugly face and a nice face. 'Which one of these two faces that you see here is ugly, and which one is nice?' She awaited the result anxiously. Kai's spindly, stooping figure appeared in the kitchen doorway; his forehead was wrinkled. 'I don't understand,' he said. 'A two-year-old child should be able to handle that, and Bent is so gifted! Maybe there is some defect in that test.'

But soon he forgot all about it and bounded down the steps to get a head of celery. You couldn't offer people cheese without celery stalks!

Even before the guests arrived, she was unable to hide her exhaustion. Her hair was limp from the steam in the kitchen; her only decent dress was tight around the middle. The energetic, perfectly made-up young women (women in that circle never studied so hard that it detracted from their looks) she let in made her feel ugly and awkward. When they had all settled in, they sat for an hour or so, smoking and chatting, and each time Lulu left the room, Kai shouted, 'Where are you going now? Relax. Stay here with us.' 'He's like a chicken without a head when you aren't in the room,' teased one of the women, while she looked at Kai with steady, beaming eyes. He was like another person. A white shirt ironed at the last second, and a rare humorous glint in his eye that she could only recall from when they were engaged. Something he never lavished on her alone. Why not? He loved her; he was dependent on her, but he also loved the endearment of others. He was like a vain child – a difficult child.

Stepping back into the living room, she blinked slightly at the light, and her gaze sought out Kai's. Now he was elated, totally happy, the center of the group's attention. He was talking non-stop, his thin fingers outlining curves in the air when he wanted to explain something. All the bottles and glasses were empty. The tablecloth was stained with red wine and gravy, the air was thick and close from the smoke. She sat down, without anyone seeming to notice. In any case, they didn't take their eyes off Kai – neither the men nor the women. She felt a sudden urge to close her eyes and go to sleep. A dark-haired woman, whom she recognized from the summer, when they had held study circles in psychology once a week, smiled at her and made room next to her on the divan. 'You look tired, Lulu,' she said sympathetically. Appalled, Lulu straightened up on her seat and smiled vacantly. 'I'm not tired at all,' she said quickly, and in the same breath, 'Isn't it great that Kai is doing so well?'

They both looked at him. Then the young woman

said warmly, 'He's smarter than any of us. It's a shame if he doesn't get the most out of his ability.'

Lulu didn't answer. Was it her fault if he didn't get the most out of his ability? Had her loving and all too fertile body pulled him down into the banal and boring? The psychoanalyst was supposed to free him from guilt, but who was going to free her? She was still looking at her husband. His thin, well-proportioned frame, his burning eyes, the words streaming from his beautifully arched lips. Yes, he was happy now, she thought; these people idolize him; he doesn't need me. And after they've left, it occurred to her, he will keep me awake the rest of the night talking about the party, and I will have to say that his friends are absolutely the most fabulous people – everything he loves I have to admire too, while also knowing that I don't measure up to them – but I am all alone with the baby I'm carrying. If he mentions it at all, it's as an increased expense – a bill from the butcher, or an oppressive creditor.

Everyone was talking all around her, over her head, and the bitterness was overflowing without her being able to stop it, filling her mind and senses with poisonous steam. She didn't understand why, and she had never felt like this before. She had always been so gracious in excusing him, and for months she had stood guard between him and the outside world. Kept her family and girlfriends at bay with all kinds of pretenses, sent friends away when they appeared at the door, endlessly empathetic: 'Is he depressed again? Dear God, what that man is up against!' She had even taken it out on Bent, when he'd been rambunctious: 'Daddy needs peace and quiet!'

This wasn't what she had imagined when they got married. But what that was, she wasn't really sure. A girlfriend had brought them together: 'A devastatingly handsome and smart guy is coming tonight; you absolutely have to meet him!'

The 'devastatingly handsome guy' was back now. He was talking with a pale young man whom Lulu didn't care for, because he always asked with such earnestness if she 'was doing well', and after an affirmative answer, would turn away with a doubtful, knowing expression, as if no one, according to his definition, could go around 'doing well'; and if it really were the case, he wasn't the least bit interested. For his part, he had the look of someone who suffered from constant indigestion; Kai was speaking to this person fervently, bent toward and directly facing him, in the way that a child is completely absorbed with something nearby. 'Psychiatrists won't acknowledge the analytical method,' he said, 'but they will have to eventually, you can bet on that. Not one of them has the least grasp of what they're dealing with.'

Lulu's bitterness congealed into a small, hard knot, there, where her heart usually sat. She stood up all of a sudden, pale, and without looking at any of the others. 'Do you mind if I head to bed? I'm exhausted,' she said, loudly and clearly, and there was a brief silence in the room. Kai finally stared at her with an angry, cold, irritated, and somewhat confused expression in his eyes.

'You're tired?' he asked, as if she had said something

unseemly, unheard of, almost indecent. Then he wrinkled his forehead and brushed his hand through his hair, bewildered, as if he were seeking aid against an injustice that had been leveled at him. The men looked at the women; the women at the men. A kind of collusion sprang up among them, brushing Lulu aside, but she held herself erect and expressionless as they stood up and said goodbye.

When the door was shut behind the last one, he turned toward her angrily. 'What the devil are you doing?' he shouted. 'Don't you have the most basic decency?' He looked like he wanted to hit her. Then he saw her face was wet with tears, slowly slipping out between her eyelashes, and he observed her a moment, full of wonder. He had never seen her cry before. Sheepishly, he led her to the divan, where she pulled close to him, shaking with sobs and exhaustion like a small animal seeking protection. He got a blanket and laid it over her. He stood up, observing her, fragile and bent. The gleam in his eye was gone, the party was over. Outside, the birds were starting to sing. He got down on one knee and caressed her hair. She took his hand and put it to her cheek, and looked up at him helplessly and inquisitively, but he gently pulled his hand back.

'We are quite a pair,' he said quietly, more to himself than to her.

PENGUIN ARCHIVE

H. G. Wells *The Time Machine*
M. R. James *The Stalls of Barchester Cathedral*
Jane Austen *The History of England by a Partial,
    Prejudiced and Ignorant Historian*
Edgar Allan Poe *Hop-Frog*
Virginia Woolf *The New Dress*
Antoine de Saint-Exupéry *Night Flight*
Oscar Wilde *A Poet Can Survive Everything But a Misprint*
George Orwell *Can Socialists be Happy?*
Dorothy Parker *Horsie*
D. H. Lawrence *Odour of Chrysanthemums*
Homer *The Wrath of Achilles*
Emily Brontë *No Coward Soul Is Mine*
Romain Gary *Lady L.*
Charles Dickens *The Chimes*
Dante *Hell*
Georges Simenon *Stan the Killer*
F. Scott Fitzgerald *The Rich Boy*
Katherine Mansfield *A Dill Pickle*
Fyodor Dostoyevsky *The Dream of a Ridiculous Man*

Franz Kafka *A Hunger-Artist*

Leo Tolstoy *Family Happiness*

Karen Blixen *The Dreaming Child*

Federico García Lorca *Cicada!*

Vladimir Nabokov *Revenge*

Albert Camus *A Short Guide to Towns Without a Past*

Muriel Spark *The Driver's Seat*

Carson McCullers *Reflections in a Golden Eye*

Wu Cheng'en *Monkey King Makes Havoc in Heaven*

Friedrich Nietzsche *Ecce Homo*

Laurie Lee *A Moment of War*

Roald Dahl *Lamb to the Slaughter*

Frank O'Connor *The Genius*

James Baldwin *The Fire Next Time*

Hermann Hesse *Strange News from Another Planet*

Gertrude Stein *Paris France*

Seneca *Why I am a Stoic*

Snorri Sturluson *The Prose Edda*

Elizabeth Gaskell *Lois the Witch*

Sei Shōnagon *A Lady in Kyoto*

Yasunari Kawabata *Thousand Cranes*

Jack Kerouac *Tristessa*

Arthur Schnitzler *A Confirmed Bachelor*

Chester Himes *All God's Chillun Got Pride*

Bram Stoker *The Burial of the Rats*
Czesław Miłosz *Rescue*
Hans Christian Andersen *The Emperor's New Clothes*
Bohumil Hrabal *Closely Watched Trains*
Italo Calvino *Under the Jaguar Sun*
Stanislaw Lem *The Seventh Voyage*
Shirley Jackson *The Daemon Lover*
Stefan Zweig *Chess*
Kate Chopin *The Story of an Hour*
Allen Ginsberg *Sunflower Sutra*
Rabindranath Tagore *The Broken Nest*
Søren Kierkegaard *The Seducer's Diary*
Mary Shelley *Transformation*
Nikolai Leskov *Night Owls*
Willa Cather *A Lost Lady*
Emilia Pardo Bazán *The Lady Bandit*
W. B. Yeats *Sailing to Byzantium*
Margaret Cavendish *The Blazing World*
Lafcadio Hearn *Some Japanese Ghosts*
Sarah Orne Jewett *The Country of the Pointed Firs*
Vincent van Gogh *For Art and for Life*
Dylan Thomas *Do Not Go Gentle Into That Good Night*
Mikhail Bulgakov *A Dog's Heart*
Saadat Hasan Manto *The Price of Freedom*

Gérard de Nerval *October Nights*
Rumi *Where Everything is Music*
H. P. Lovecraft *The Shadow Out of Time*
Christina Rossetti *To Read and Dream*
Dambudzo Marechera *The House of Hunger*
Andy Warhol *Beauty*
Maurice Leblanc *The Escape of Arsène Lupin*
Eileen Chang *Jasmine Tea*
Irmgard Keun *After Midnight*
Walter Benjamin *Unpacking My Library*
Epictetus *Whatever is Rational is Tolerable*
Ota Pavel *How I Came to Know Fish*
César Aira *An Episode in the Life of a Landscape Painter*
Hafez *I am a Bird from Paradise*
Clarice Lispector *The Burned Sinner
    and the Harmonious Angels*
Maryse Condé *Tales from the Heart*
Audre Lorde *Coal*
Mary Gaitskill *Secretary*
Tove Ditlevsen *The Umbrella*
June Jordan *Passion*
Antonio Tabucchi *Requiem*
Alexander Lernet-Holenia *Baron Bagge*
Wang Xiaobo *The Maverick Pig*